LIFE BEHIND MY JOURNEY

LuKesha Tate

LuKesha Tate

Email: Creationluz@gmail.com

ISBN: 978-1-7358024-1-1 (Paperback)
ISBN: 978-1-7358024-2-8 (e-book)

Front cover image by Artist.
Book design by Bianca Brown.
Edited by Katherine A. Young
(Email: info@katherineayoung.com)

Printed by Write It Out Publishing LLC as Contributor in the United States of America.

First printing edition 2020. Word Count: 25,100

Table of Contents

Dedication

This book is dedicated to everyone seeking healing from life experiences of abused relationships. To people who are willing to allow God, to redirect their journey after the process and knowing there is love within you to move forward.

Preface

Did they care about me when they would abuse
me mentally, emotionally, physically?
Manipulation and Deceiver?
I've learned to listen.
I wouldn't have ever thought it would have
happened to me.
Not me!

"Verbal abuse is harsher than physical abuse;
insulting language directed at a person someone
repeatedly uses words to demean, frighten, or
use clichés in sentences" is not LOVE.

About the Author

LuKesha Tate is the oldest sibling of four children. A pivotal point in her life occurred when she gave birth to her beautiful daughter in 1991 as a Freshmen in high school. In order to stay focused on her studies, her mother quit her job and helped care for her daughter so that she could complete school from Kenwood Academy High School in 1994. LuKesha then attended Kennedy King College with the intention of becoming a nurse, until she decided to birth a nonprofit organization entitled Better Sister Growth Network in 2012. The organization is now known as Better Sister and Brother Growth Network where the focus is all about strengthening, empowering, and equipping low-income families and individuals. The organization offers services to the community to help with basic needs, economic workforce development, and it also serves as a resource center for domestic violence victims in the Chicagoland, South Suburbs Illinois and Northwest Indiana areas. In addition, LuKesha also birthed Tate's Writing Service Agency, LLC, which assists nonprofit organizations and business owners with grant funding, as well as mentoring entrepreneurs throughout the United States. Ms. Tate is the author of *Tate's Grant Writing Manual: Step by Step of Understanding How to Get*

Funded! (www.amazon.com). You may learn more about LuKesha Tate at https://tatesgrantwriter.com/.

LIFE BEHIND MY JOURNEY

LuKesha Tate

CHAPTER ONE: Growing Up

There's a moment as a young girl growing up that you realize the pressure's mounting. Being the eldest brings immeasurable expectations from your younger siblings and other family members. I've heard plenty stories of similar families that were poor and struggled. We may have been one of those families, but my mother worked hard with two jobs to supply us with whatever needs we desired. Although my family has had our share of issues, I never felt unloved or alone.

Now somewhere in this beautiful story, as a little girl with all of this love, it seems I've grown into a teenager—that is still missing something. It's like there's a gap in my soul that's awaiting fulfillment. It wasn't long until I found what I was missing: my biological father in my life, even though three men who was a great part of my life showered me with affection, protection, and lots of love. I soon learned that I didn't have the same father as my siblings. My family had desperately tried to keep this secret from me.

I was shocked, disappointed, and hurt to find out that I had a different father, and I spent hours going over the details in a book, found by my siblings' and me. It was hidden inside of a closet that had baby memories with my name on the book. I approached my parents to ask them about the lies within this book. It was difficult for me to

even build up the strength to confront my parents at such a young age. It was even harder for them to tell me what I needed to hear. The tears rolled down my face like acid burning through my heart. Feelings of straight-up betrayal consumed me as the rage enveloped my body with my parents every deceitful admission.
Are they serious?

Of course, the details about my biological father mattered. But these are things I should have known all along.

How dare they?

I couldn't believe the things that they were saying. I had a right to meet this person who they claimed rejected me. Maybe they believed they were doing what was best for me... but really wasn't. Could he explain how he could reject a child that didn't ask to be a part of this world? What does he look like? Do I have other family? Is this the reason why I don't look like my siblings? When will I get to meet him? I needed to know more. When I did get the opportunity to speak to him, years later, he really didn't have much to say. He didn't even ask one question about me. I was so disappointed...rejected...hurt. This man I personified throughout my childhood and waited to meet was a huge disappointment.

There was no connection. No connection from the one person I deserved a relationship with. But it really just doesn't matter at this point. The communication with him wasn't what I expected. I was looking for a fairy tale. It was clear that my mother wasn't lying about this man, and I wasn't missing anything.

Somewhere inside of me, I'm sure my life's journey began with my non-existent biological father, and the search of a man to replace my fairytale. Why couldn't I just focus on what I had in the three men that raised me? The rejection and pain of my father's dismissal still lives within me. Although every part of my being wants to move on from that, I just can't find the will.

Unfortunately, that hole he has drilled within me will continue to affect my relationships...and later in my life's journey.

CHAPTER TWO: A Girl Becoming A Woman

Let's begin at the age of thirteen. I had begun to explore my body. Laying in my bed, I had shut my eyes closed. I slowly began to move my hands around my breasts then slowly starting down to my vagina area, I spread open my legs widely, starting to move my fingers over my pubic hair area, sliding my fingers in and out of my vagina, thinking to myself *This feels so good.* Noises began to flow out of my mouth, and I was thinking to myself *I have to be quiet—my little sister was sleeping in the other bed.* I couldn't help it—it felt so good. And then I got this hot sensation over my body and my bed was completely wet. What could this be? Where did I learn this from? What was this called? I couldn't dare tell my mother, that I was doing this to myself…she would kill me. How embarrassing. It felt too good to stop and I continued doing this every night until…

I met Shawn when I was fourteen at the time. I was hanging out at a friend's house when she was visiting her mom. It wasn't love at first sight; it simply was his smile that got my attention. At such a young age, I wouldn't even know what love was. It wasn't what I've heard how you're going to know that that's "The One." It was just in passing where we locked eyes. Sounds like something out of a fairy tale story, right?

The next day at school, my friend mentioned to me that someone wanted to meet me. I'm assuming it was Shawn; we had locked eyes in just that quick of a passing moment. I had explained to my friend that my mother would never allow me to have a friend as a boy. This would be the hardest hook-up ever; I had never lied to my mom. I wasn't allowed to hang out on a school night nor spend nights out; this would have to have been the worst lie ever. My friend told my mother that her mother was extremely sick, and she would like for me to go with her to visit. My mother agreed. We couldn't believe the lie worked.

Since I had agreed to hook up with Shawn, everything was planned. We went down to my friend's house and there he was standing in the hallway, smiling at me. Immediately, I knew that this hook-up was dangerous, but I couldn't turn back now. I'm here now; it was like a rush of feelings going through my body. I stood waiting patiently, not knowing the danger of hanging in the hallway of the projects. Shawn had come over to talk to me; his voice was of concern. He explained the dangers of being out late and how he didn't want me to continue waiting on him. He gave me his "beeper number" and a code, which would let him know it was me calling.

As we were on the bus going home, I couldn't do anything but just keep going over the sound of Shawn's voice in my mind. I totally forgot about my friend ever being on the bus with me. I had so much anticipation of getting home to "beep" him; surely, I wasn't thinking about what I would tell my mother if a boy called the house. That lie would come later. What I did know was that I wouldn't dare let her know anything about Shawn or how I met him. If my mother did find out, I knew that I would no longer be able to hang out with my friend.

Honestly, this secret would soon lead to something unacceptable, and I knew it wasn't going to be good. How was I going to pull the telephone calls off? This is where the start of my manipulation would begin. My friend would call the house at a certain time after school, and she would "three-way call" Shawn, wait until he picked up, and then she would hang-up the telephone. Sometimes, she would just put the telephone down until we finished talking.

Unfortunately, these phone calls ended up backfiring in my face with my so-called friend. One major lesson I learned from my friend conducting these "three-way" calls was to "never allow friends to know about your boyfriend or man." I was young and didn't have a clue about boys, or betrayal of a friendship either.

That's a whole other story to come about my friend and Shawn's relationship. CONTINUING ON...

I finally got to talk to Shawn alone, since this particular weekend night, my friend had something else to do. I took a risk, and it was such a great conversation. I had learned a lot about him: he was much older and he attended Dunbar High School; he had three siblings; and we even talked about his relationship with his father and mother. Our talk went on throughout the night. I couldn't stop blushing and laughing all night long. As our conversation was ending, we had discussed how we were going to see one another again; we knew we would have to get my friend onboard.

Plans were all in place and we were ready to go. My friend was onboard as my back-up. It was getting closer to the summer break, nearing time for us to graduate eighth grade. We had early dismissal at school, our parents were at work, and the meeting location "of course" was Shawn's house. It was perfect planning. I didn't have a clue what I was getting myself into. I'm thinking to myself: *Kesha girl; he's much older, sex is all on his mind.*

I didn't have anyone to tell me about what boys wanted. My friend was the only one and she slept around a lot. Her advice was not the best advice. All I could think about was my mother telling me boys were nasty, and that they just wanted what was between your legs.

Huh: Lady, that made no sense to me. I wouldn't dare have asked my father for advice. In his eyes, I was his precious jewel. As I'm walking through the playground heading to his building, I see Shawn looking out the window for me. Nervousness is taking over, not knowing what to expect out of this day alone with a "man" because he most certainly was not a boy. As I entered the elevator, I kept telling myself that everything was going to be alright, but my heart was making me feel otherwise.

The doors open and Shawn was standing waiting on me, smiling. I follow him into the apartment. The door slams closed. Do you know how PROJECT doors sound? Like when they shut, it's just ABSOLUTE and no way to go back. That's how my heart was feeling: I'm here now. No turning around.

Actually, it wasn't a bad first date. I was thinking the worst, or maybe I was expecting other things to happen, listening to my friend. Shawn ordered lunch, and we talked and laughed the entire time. Then in the next moment, he leaned in to kiss me, and my reaction was to turn my face. I had been watching television shows, rehearsed this moment in my head; I wanted to see how this kiss would feel. I closed my eyes, and it was wet. Hold up—a tongue? Wait. Wait—why the tongue? This wasn't on television. It felt sloppy, but the more we kept doing this French kissing, I became good at it. The evening was ending; I had to be home at a certain time. Shawn walked me to the bus stop, we kissed goodbye, and I was to "beep" him once I made it home.

As soon as I arrived home, I immediately went into the bathroom, removed my pants and laid on the floor. I needed to release that pent-up feeling. I closed my eyes and pictured Shawn kissing me, and I placed my fingers inside of my vagina. A hot sensation exploded out of my body...wetness everywhere. It felt so good to release that feeling—I still don't know what this was called, and I dare not tell anyone, because it seemed like I was so embarrassing. I had to hurry and clean myself up before my mother wanted to know what was going on in the bathroom. I went into my room and "beeped" Shawn. I couldn't wait until we saw each other again. It was just a matter of time.

Eighth-grade graduation was coming up, and my

mother still had no clue about Shawn. I wanted him to attend my graduation; the only person that I knew wouldn't mind was my father, and he's the only human being that could make some sense out of it to my mother.

It's the weekend, and my siblings and I were at my father's apartment. I kinda mentioned to my father and stepmother Shawn's name, very little detail about him, and how I've met his mother. I explained to them both how I would like for him to attend my graduation. *Of course,* my father says, "Let's meet him first before I decide to bring this conversation to your mother." But what you'll understand later is that this was a bad idea without involving my mother from the beginning. I let Shawn know about the meeting with my father and stepmother, and he was very confident that things would go well. I wasn't shocked that my father and stepmother liked Shawn when they met him, which further made me think that if they liked him so much, what's the harm in allowing him to attend my graduation? My father reassured me things would work out fine with my mother. *Man is you serious?* is all I can think as though my father forgot my mother's personality.

Soon after my father and stepmother met Shawn, I arrived home from school to see my parents waiting for me on the sofa. *Oh boy!* The look in my mother's eyes was like flames of fire and frustration. As I sat down in-between my parent's, my father reassured me once again that everything was going to be fine, and that my mother just wanted to know a little bit about the young man. With excitement in my voice, I began to tell her all of the nice things about Shawn, but not too many details. She's not saying anything. I can't feel her out except to know her body language was horrible. I realized this lady was only allowing him to come to the graduation because of my father. I got up from the sofa, gave my father a big hug, and headed towards my bedroom.

As I'm heading to my bedroom, I could hear hollering and yelling. My mother was so angry at my father for allowing this to happen. She was screaming, "How could you allow this to happen? You let Shawn come over to your apartment without discussing things with me?"

Calmly, my father said, "She'll be alright, nothing's going to happen. it's just a graduation ceremony." The next couple of days, my mother didn't speak to me, and I knew she was disappointed and wanted more from me. I was her oldest—I should have "known better." It truly hurt me that my mother wasn't talking to me, but I knew this would happen once she found out about me having a "boyfriend." My parents thought this was a phase of having a "boyfriend" and it would pass. If only they knew...

Graduation Day finally arrived. I'm super-duper excited. My parents, family, and Shawn would all be there for my big day. As I walked across the stage with excitement from receiving my diploma, all I could think about was *How were they getting along with Shawn? Was my mother being nice?* The ceremony had ended, and I walked outside of the building and everyone's waiting on me to take pictures. As my mother handed me flowers, before I knew it, I asked if we went out to eat, could Shawn come as well.

Silence. No one's talking anymore or laughing. All

of a sudden, I saw my father, mother, and family get into a huddle. My mother burst out and said, "After we eat, we'll discuss that."

At dinner, question after question darted towards Shawn. It was driving me crazy. He was so calm, answering every question that came his way with confidence. I couldn't help but smile; he had such a charm about himself. Then I heard my mother say, "Alright, hang out with Shawn and your best friend, and be home by 7:00 p.m."

My father quickly perked up. "Why not 9 p.m.? She deserved to stay out until curfew; she's in high school now." If only my mother could have stabbed my father with her eyes, she would have. She icily agreed to 9:00 p.m. My mother wasn't happy at all. We had planned to go see a movie. Of course, plans had changed: the time-frame I was on didn't allow enough time for us to finish a movie. So, we ended up back at our elementary school sitting in the playground talking all night, holding hands and making plans to see each other again.

It would be a day that my mother was at work, my

siblings were with our father, and I would say that I was cramping. We talked about the code I would use when everyone was out of the house. I couldn't wait until we could be alone. I wanted to feel what my friend was explaining to me as "good." Still, no one knew that I was making myself feel good. I was still too ashamed to tell anybody what I was doing.

It was a hot summer day, and the sun was shining bright. I used the code "007" when I "beeped" Shawn, letting him know "nobody is home." My heart was pounding; my vagina was throbbing and very moist. I took a shower, put on clean panties, having the expectation of knowing I was about to lose my virginity to Shawn. Was this right? NO. But I was so curious, I wanted to know how it felt. Would it hurt? Would he make me feel like I make myself feel? Now, this may sound crazy. My friend told me I would experience pain, and blood would gush out and then afterwards, it would feel so good. Why in the world would I still want to do this after hearing all of that? Either way, I wanted to have sex. Was it worth the pain and blood? Welp, I was about to find out.

The phone rang, and Shawn was downstairs. I buzzed him into the building. My heart would not stop pounding...I was so nervous. I kept walking back and forth, peeping out the hole in the door, nervously waiting in the hallway of the house. Two knocks on the door, and I invited him in. We went into the living room, watched some television, talking and laughing. Shawn asked me what time I was expecting everyone back, and I let him know we didn't have a lot of time.

Swiftly, he moved in closer towards me and we began to kiss. I started getting warm and moist, and it's feeling so good. He asked me to show him my room. Hesitantly I said, "I'm not ready yet. Let's not do this...let's wait until another day." He reassured me that it wasn't going to hurt. He promised to be gentle. I told him about all the horrible stories I've heard, and he laughed. "It will only be a little blood. I will take my time," he said as he then grabbed my hand, asked me to show him my room and he told me we needed a towel.

I removed my clothes and laid down on my back

with the stiff towel underneath me on my bed. I watched Shawn as he removed his clothes. We never took our eyes off each other. Shawn climbed on top of me, kissing my body all over. He made me feel so comfortable. I closed my eyes. Then I felt something forceful, painful, entering my vagina. With a sudden cry, I asked him to stop. He kept telling me to relax, and that I'd hear a popping sound soon. Huh? What popping sound? He's moaning: it's good to him. I couldn't stop crying. "Please," I begged, "please,"—then a "POP" sounded in the air. Blood was everywhere on the towel. *Oh no! I'm never doing this again!*

Who was I fooling? This was my first experience, but it wasn't going to be the last time. We had to rush to get everything cleaned up. I couldn't look at him; he kept apologizing telling me that the next time would be better. Though this may sound silly or crazy, I couldn't wait until the next time, just like how my friend always told me that the second time was going to be much better.

Summer break was ending. It was almost time for school to begin: Freshman year in high school.

Things had been great with Shawn: the sex indescribable; his kisses; sucking; "eating"—I didn't even know what that was until Shawn began to explain that's a way a man showed his affection by making a woman feel good sexually. I'm a *Woman* now? I'm just a pre-teen going to high school. Could he be right? Am I a woman? Soon I was most definitely going to learn about what a "woman" was all about, who lived inside of a pre-teen's body.

Something was going on with my body: my nipples were sore; I had zero energy, and I was vomiting every day. And now, no menstrual cycle. What was I going to do? I couldn't tell my mother. So, I expressed these symptoms to Shawn. He laughed. I'm confused as to why he was laughing. "You're pregnant."

PREGNANT. Wait. Hold up. I couldn't even process what was coming out of his mouth. I saw his mouth moving, and I thought I heard him clearly. We were about to have a baby. I am shocked. I can't think right now. I can't believe this is happening. I'm crying. Shawn tells me to not worry because he's going to help me. He's going to take care of his child and me. Has he just lost his mind? My mother was going to kill me, Shawn, and the baby. What was I going to do? I needed to talk to my father—he'd understand.

As the months were passing by us, Shawn stuck to his words. My stomach was getting bigger, and I still hadn't told my mother and father. The only people I felt comfortable telling were my siblings, since we kept secrets amongst one another. They didn't care—but I knew that I'd have to reveal this to my family soon. I didn't know how a baby was supposed to come out of me, so I began to read a lot at the public library. I had no prenatal care and no vitamins. What was I going to do?

Shawn had already told his mother, and she was excited, busy buying baby clothes. "Baby clothes?" Hold on. I hadn't even had the guts to tell my mother, father, or the rest of my family. This had to be done soon; I couldn't keep going straight into my room after school, wearing big clothes to hide my belly.

My mother was lying in her bedroom as it was her

day off. All I kept saying to myself was *Jesus, give me the strength and please don't let her kill me.* This had to be the night I told her because I couldn't keep hiding, listening to my friend, Shawn, and his mother. I had been reading all of these books, taking all kinds of things to kill this child in my stomach and I had tried remedies of sticking foreign objects inside of me (coat hangers and tampons). *Jesus!* I needed help to get this baby out of me, before I destroyed myself. I nervously walked into my mother's bedroom, and all of a sudden, it felt cold. "Mom, I have something to tell you." She looked at me. I couldn't quite get the words out, so I hurriedly jumbled them out. "I'm pregnant."

Nothing. She said nothing. All of a sudden, she removed her bed sheet, slid out of her bed and stood by her bedside and said steely, "What did you say?"
I repeated myself. "I'm pregnant." She walked towards me as I began to back into her master bathroom. I saw her mouth, but I couldn't quite hear her yelling. Out of nowhere, she knocked me right into the bathtub. She pulled me up as she's yelling "Call Shawn right now!" I dialed his

house phone number.

"Shawn, my mother—" I briefly said when the telephone was snatched out of my hand. I was crying uncontrollably as my mother was yelling at Shawn through the receiver. After I don't know how long, Shawn's mother got on the phone. They're talking. I couldn't hear much because everything was a blur as voices were fading out. Next thing I knew, my mother yelled "Go get your shit—we're going to the hospital."

On a school night, we arrived at the Cook County Hospital. I was exhausted and relieved at the same time. My "secret" was no longer a secret. I could see the hurt in my mother's eyes; she looked like she was holding back a river of tears. My mother was strong—the whole ride to the hospital, she never said anything to me. As night was going into the morning, my name was finally called in the Waiting area for an exam. I was praying they didn't find out the things I'd been doing to myself.

The doctor returned to the room, explained to my mother how far along I was, and to follow up with the clinic to make an appointment for prenatal care. My mother told the doctor "Oh no—she's getting an abortion." I didn't have a clue what an abortion was; the doctor explained to my mother the dangers of an abortion, and that I was too far along—five months to be exact—for this option. My mother was adamant about her decision. As we got into the car, I asked her what an abortion was. Shortly, her reply was "It's something you're going to have." She'd explain it to my father, family, and then I was no longer allowed to see Shawn once the procedure was done. She then went on to tell me all of the bad things Shawn was doing for my future, and how a child would destroy all of the things I wanted to do.

Completely exhausted from the late night at the hospital and not making it home until almost 2 a.m., still forced to attend school, when I arrived back home after school, my father was seated on the couch with my mother. I'm thinking *Here we go, whatever this abortion thing is, let's just get it over with.* My father and mother had this long speech with me, and they explained how they had spoken to the entire family and scraped up all this money to get an abortion and how far the ride was from Chicago. I agreed because I just wanted to get this all over with. I called Shawn to let him know what the plan was, and it's clear he was not happy with the decision. He's mad at me for not speaking up. I'm confused as I explained to Shawn that I didn't want a baby. I'm just a baby myself. I didn't know how to raise a baby. Shawn went off, yelling through the receiver telling me he'd be there for me and how his mother was very disappointed. This was my body, my life, and I was going to have the procedure. The appointment was made.

This drive was one of the longest drives I've ever had. I'm so glad that my mother was talking to me, though I knew it was because my father was riding with us. She really hadn't been speaking to me since the night I told her I was pregnant. My father looked at me and explained his true feelings: he wasn't happy about the choice my mother has made, and he felt as though she influenced my decision. To be honest, she really hasn't. I was trying to abort the child on my own.

As we arrived at the location, I felt this horrible

feeling inside of me. I couldn't explain it, but it just was not right. We arrived in the waiting area. Shortly after, my name was called for an examination. The doctor called my parents into the room. He explained to them about a three-day procedure that they would have to perform due to me being so far along. The procedure would consist of them having to insert needles into my cervix in order to dilate me as if I was going into labor. The danger of the procedure would either kill me or I wouldn't be able to have any more children in the future. "Hold up," my father says. "I will not allow my baby girl to go through no such thing."

"I don't want her life messed up," my mother bleakly stated.
My parents thanked the doctor for being honest. The ride home was horrible. Silence. Thoughts ran through my mind: *If only I would've told my parents earlier. LuKesha, you was a girl, but now you're about to become a "woman."*

When we went home, I made the call to let Shawn know the news. "Guess what? We're having a baby." Time was moving rapidly. Doctor appointments every month. School assignments were killing me. Then there was pressure from the high school I was attending because they didn't want me being a bad impression for my classmates and wanted me to stay home. They didn't want my peers to think it was alright to be pregnant as a freshman in high school.

Well, come to find out, I wasn't the only one in my freshman class expecting a baby. Both Shawn and my mother went to the Board of Education and found out as long as we were excelling in school, we had all rights to attend high school.

The school year went great. I did excel and I was going into my Sophomore year. Hello summer break. I was eight months pregnant and expected to drop this baby any moment now. Doctor appointments were every week. The closer I got to having my baby, the more excited I was to see her face, hold her, and kiss her. I hadn't really saw Shawn. Things between us weren't working out. I was maturing in this process of carrying my little girl, and Shawn wasn't any help. Sex was overrated. I needed him to be mature. We were expecting a baby that depended completely on us, expecting love—just like I was.

July 18, 1991: I sat in the doctor's office anxious, scared, and in pain. My name was called to go back to the exam room. After my doctor examined me, he said "Yep—it's time."

"Excuse me?" I said with surprise.
He said, "Gather all of your belongings, walk over to the hospital building. When you get there, they will be expecting you. So, check-in and I'll see you over there." As I was walking into the waiting room, the nurse was already explaining all of the details to my mother. Mom looked at me and said, "It's time for the baby to come." Instantly, I couldn't hear her once again; it seemed as if I went through this phase where I blocked people's voices out. I began to laugh out loud and my mother blankly stared at me. Then I heard her calling my name, asking, "Where's Shawn? Or his mother?" I snapped out of it.

"Mother, just call Shawn and his mother and let them know please." I'm in pain, but I tried to remain calm. I'm checked in at the hospital. It seemed as if everything was moving extremely fast. I've been told things aren't going well with me and the baby. All I could remember hearing was my mother screaming, "Save my daughter! She can always have another baby."

It felt like I was in and out of consciousness. The anesthesiologist gave me an epidural injection for the pain. I heard the nurse say, "Tell her not to move or she'll be paralyzed." My mother was holding me so tight. I saw Shawn and his mother faces' smiling. I heard my doctor: "You're doing so well LuKesha. She's almost here and everything will be over. Then you can hold her." I smiled and was unconscious again. All of a sudden, the doctor and nurses rushed me onto a delivery table. I heard my doctor: "LuKesha, if you can hear, me squeeze the nurse's hand." I couldn't feel anything. I saw unfamiliar faces telling me to push or she'll die. I couldn't push. I felt so numb. Then out of nowhere, I gave a big push and there she was crying, wet, covered in blood. I began to cry thanking the Lord. My baby had arrived.

Welcome baby girl: July 19, 1991. She's such a beautiful sight to see.

CHAPTER THREE: Suppression of My First Love

Fast forward years later and I'm somewhere around my late twenties. *How did I get here?* That's the question I asked myself. Well, let's see: hanging out night after night in this lounge on the South-side that stayed opened until 5 a.m. My best friend, friends, and I wouldn't miss a weekend. We lived for this life. We looked forward to going shopping and finding something sexy to wear every weekend. I know it may seem immature, but to us, that's all we had. When we walked into this lounge, literally all eyes were on us: we made heads turn, men and women alike. We were known at the bar. We would always make this particular place the last stop of the night. There was so much action, jam-packed every weekend, with crowds of people standing in line—using both the front and back entrances just to get in.

It was a Saturday night, and I'm looking good, feeling sexy. Me and the girls had some drinks as we were getting ready, and even smoked a little before leaving the house. Now we were ready to hit up our normal spot. I just knew deep down inside of me that this was going to be a great night. Someone's going to catch my eye. The DJ was playing all of the right music; the atmosphere was right, and the drinks were good...and the men were looking mighty tasty.

There he was: Hazel-brown Eye'z, dark complexion, short and fine. I never seemed to find short men attractive, but he caught my eyes. I just knew I had to have him. Sounds like something out of a fairy tale book, right? Body language said a lot and I'm a big flirt. His friend came over to ask my girlfriend something, they began to talk, laugh, and so forth. Of course, I pretended like he wasn't noticeable, even though he was standing right next to me, smelling like something out of the cologne store, wearing all black from head-to-toe. In the back of my mind, I couldn't wait for him to start talking to me. Suddenly, this deep voice comes out of this man's mouth asking me to dance. I had no plans to turn him down, but at the same time, I didn't want him to think I was desperate. I had been waiting on this moment all night! Once we started dancing that was it! Uh-hum! Great dancer, and his eye contact was remarkable. Our bodies were talking with the sound of the music, and as the night went on, we had conversation after conversation. He was so charming and funny. We exchanged phone numbers before the night could end.

The telephone rang the next day, and as I answered, I blushed when I heard that deep voice saying, "Hello beautiful." Instantly, my body caught a hot sensation just from hearing his voice. It definitely made me feel some type of way. Even though I wasn't expecting the call, in a sense, I knew he would call. It was funny because my best friend had mentioned that I should be expecting his call very soon. However, that night we met at the lounge, we had what felt like an endless conversation, with lots of laughter, getting to know each other and finding out we shared the same Scorpio sign.

We were alike, but different in so many ways. As the night was coming to an end, and early signs of morning broke in the dusk, we had noticed the time and how much we laughed over the course of the night. We just couldn't believe we had talked that much. Before we hung up, we planned to meet up this upcoming weekend for drinks and another dance. It was unbelievable as I hung up the telephone. To actually talk all night with a man…now that's a "turn on."

After our first conversation over the telephone, we had started talking every day, learning so many things about each other. It all felt so perfect. I felt like he was going to be a great match for me. He was family orientated; he had goals, and he was a man that was rooted and grounded.

Back at the spot, hanging out with our friends having drinks, dancing the night away, me and Eye'z weren't into nobody else but each other the whole night. I wasn't expecting things to turn out this well, based on how we met. You kiss a frog, and he may become a prince. The night was over and Eye'z goes home with me. Yes, I'm expecting sex. I've been drinking, smoking a little—the chemistry was right. I have my own place, my daughter was gone, and my friend didn't need a place to have sex. Everything was all good. We arrived at my apartment around 3 a.m. I'm ready—so ready, that I was disappointed. Nothing happened because Eye'z was a straight gentleman. I'm thinking to myself *Girl, stop being a whore, dropping your panties when every dick comes your way.* The night was going great as we're talking, touching and he hits me with an interesting request. "Can I give you a full body massage naked?"

"Naked?" I sighed. "Why not?" Especially how things were going between us.

Slowly, my clothes came off, he's watching me, and the eye contact was intensifying. I've never experienced this feeling: not touching anyone, where I felt uncomfortable, but also comfortable the more he's making me feel like he wanted me in a good way. I laid down on the couch. His hands were warm, soft and gentle. He kissed the back of my neck. His tongue went up and down my spine. I closed my eyes. I felt as if he's taking me somewhere mentally, stimulating me all at the same time. I fell asleep—laughing.

I awoke to another day— with a blanket covering

my body, thinking *What just happened to me? Did this man drug me? Did he rape me?* I wasn't sore and I didn't feel sluggish. So, where's Eye'z? I got up, checked my bedroom, checked the front door, and I looked out the window. His car was gone.

No Eye'z. I sat down on the couch, looked on the table and he left a note saying he enjoyed the night, he's gone home, and he'll see me soon. Now that's a real smooth player move. Something you would see right off the movie screen.

Who would have ever thought I would begin to fall for someone like this? Well, it happened. Not only did this kind of night happen again, but it took place for at least two to four months before Eye'z decided to have sex with me. I thought he didn't find me attractive. (Side note: Ladies: A man doesn't have to have sex with you on the first night he meets you to find you attractive.) It took me time to realize that. I was vulnerable with low self-esteem and that's how he truly trapped hold of me by stimulating my mind. I was in love.

The minutes, hours, days, weeks, and months were going by so fast. I was in a relationship. Eye'z has become my friend, companion, and lover. We began to encourage one another. Eye'z was pursuing his rapping career, and I was finishing up school. No more dancing for me. I wanted to be a great girlfriend, and he has been the best person to have come into my life, besides my daughter. I had someone that made me laugh and smile. We enjoyed hanging out with our friends; we went to the movies and dinners; and we spent time with family and our kids' together. What more could I have asked for?

New Year's Eve. I'm unsure about the year, but this was a good starting point. We're all hanging out over at Eye'z' studio-apartment, and all of our friends and family are there. We had food, music, card games, and lots of liquor. I'm sick as ever, throwing up, and am in lots of pain. I can't remember what number pregnancy this was— yes, you read right: over the course of our relationship, I had terminated so many pregnancies. Don't judge me. He said he was not ready for a family.

Why didn't we use protection? I know, all of it makes sense, but don't act like you've always used protection. He has two children and I have one. He's trying to get his rap career off the ground. Even though I'm successful in making money, I just want him to be happy. If children aren't apart of the story right now, we're good.

The night was going great... until his beeper kept going off. It's very noticeable. I asked him about it and he seemed to ignore me. I asked again and he told me, "I'll get to it later." I didn't think anything of it, since it's New Year's Eve. The ball just dropped in Times Square, and it could have been his children wanting to wish him a "Happy New Year" or his parents. But he'll get to it later.

Yeah, the ball has really begun to drop—in our lives, that is. Happy New Year. We're into the beginning of the year. I'm feeling horrible, constantly vomiting, feeling more ill as each day passes. I needed to find out how far I am and soon. I get the great news that I'm carrying twins. I'm excited this New Year. New bundles of joy. Things are looking good for us.

Eye'z was off in Atlanta getting a contract signed for his music. I'm finishing up nursing school plus working. This was the right time around for us. I wanted to keep our babies. I just haven't shared the news with him, since he's away on business. I felt it's the time to share with him. I understand he'd be gone a lot, but I could handle it.

I've been constantly calling Eye'z since he'd been gone to Atlanta on supposed business these past few weeks. No answer. I really wanted to share the great news. I understood that he may have been extremely busy probably celebrating, signing contracts, meeting managers and rappers—all the things you see on television. I wanted to hear all about it. I had been leaving lots of voicemail messages, 911 beeps and I even called the hotel. No answer. I'm trying to remain calm and not think crazy thoughts as they began running through my mind. Who was he with? What female was in his room? *You haven't even gotten the money yet, and you're acting real stupid. Oh, when I finally do talk to him, I'm going to curse him out.*

The next day, my phone rang and as I looked at

the caller ID, I saw it was Eye'z. Hmm. I almost considered not answering the call, but of course, I answered anyways. What's the first thing he said? "Oh Baby, I'm so sorry, we've been in the studio all night and morning making beats. I didn't want to stop the flow and answer the telephone." Like a fool, I fell for the okey-doke and believed his lies. I later learned that's all he gave me were a bunch of lies. I asked him, "What happened at the big meeting with your manager?"

"Oh, we're having dinner tonight with a big recording company." Then I heard a voice calling him. The voice sounded like a female. I asked him who was that calling him. Eye'z rushed: "Oh baby, that's my brother telling me to hurry up and get dressed. We have that big meeting tonight and we can't be late." Quickly, Eye'z said, "I love you. I'll call you later." Before I could say anything else, he hung up. Now wasn't that some fishy business?

It was so disappointing. I was so interested in his business, that I didn't even tell him about the babies. I guess I'd have to wait until he returned back to Chicago. That's when I'd also deal with the voice I heard. It's the weekend and Eye'z has arrived home from ATL. I haven't heard from him since he acted all stupid over the phone. Plus, I've been extremely sick and working like crazy, to even deal with his mess. When I got home, all I could manage to do was cook, help my daughter with homework, and sleep.

My energy was zapped. When Eye'z finally arrived home, he didn't come to our apartment; instead, he went to his studio apartment. Something smelled fishy and looked guilty. The first person he should have seen was me. When he does finally call, the tone in his voice over the phone sounded disappointed. In his deep voice he sulked, "I need you."

"Why?" He explained that the trip to ATL wasn't good. They didn't get anyone to sign them, and none of the meetings went as planned. I'm silently thinking *Now I can't tell him about the twins.* I wouldn't want to disappoint him now or put more on him than he could handle. So, once again I had to wait until the time was right.

As I got into my car, all I could do was cry

because now, I felt like I couldn't keep my babies. When I finally arrived at Eye'z' studio-apartment, he came outside to sit in the car to talk to me about his trip. I asked him, "Why aren't we inside?"

"Ah, the fellas inside making beats." I shrugged my shoulders. He turned to me: "I'm sorry baby, what did you have to tell me?"

"Oh nothing," trying to hide my disappointment. "I'll just wait until another time. You have enough on your mind." Something was not feeling right, and everything was beginning to sound very funny. I thought to myself, *Stay calm*. I waited until the very next day, because I knew that something was wrong. Eye'z was acting too strange the day before.

I decided I would pay him an unannounced visit. It's about 6 a.m. I got into my car, but before I left, I called my baby sister and let her know where I was going. This visit felt like déjà vu. I've been here before—I know God gave us signs. I wasn't listening to God's voice. All I knew was that I was pregnant, and this nigga was lying. I'm very emotional right now and there's about to be a problem.

As I'm approaching the building, the door wasn't locked. It's cracked open like someone was expecting me to come over. I walked up the stairs to the first floor. I knocked on the door, and the door opened just like a damn movie (déjà vu)! A petite young lady said, "Hello Kesha, I've been waiting on you." In shock, I asked where was Eye'z. She swung open the door for me to walk in, standing in her t-shirt and no panties. I'm thinking to myself *Where's the music studio?* I didn't see anything that looked like a studio. I pushed open the first bedroom door. There he was laying in the bed sound asleep with a small newborn baby in his arms. I instantly snapped out. Here it was I'm pregnant, but Eye'z was lying in bed with another woman's child. Every time I got pregnant; my babies had to be aborted.

I looked at the fish aquarium that was right above his head. I saw the bat that was by the bedroom door. All I could think was *Walk over, grab the bat, and call his name.* "Eye'z." Instantly, he awoke. All I heard was "KESHAAAAA! Nooo!" I didn't even think about the baby laying there. I blanked out.

I threw back my arms and swung with all my strength. I broke the fish aquarium. Water and glass began to stream out. I snapped out for a second when I heard the young lady scream "Grab our baby!"

"Our baby?" I said. Water streamed everywhere. I began to swing the bat at him. Eye'z grabbed the bat and says, "Kesha, NO." All of a sudden, this big black woman came out of nowhere—his sister. She tried to grab me or probably swing on me. I heard Eye'z say, "No, she's pregnant!"

I'm screaming: "Why do you give a FUCK!" My sister was running in yelling: "What's going on?" She's calling my name, saying "Let's go." From that point on, I don't even remember how I got out of the situation without going to jail.

What a nightmare. Now what am I going to do? Pregnant with twins, I couldn't go back to stripping right now. I couldn't tell anyone—

especially my best friend because she was too judgmental. I'm sick every day throwing up everything I ate and drank. I couldn't even hold water or blood. Something was really wrong. I needed an appointment. I couldn't tell my mother. I had no choice but to answer Eye'z telephone calls, with his stupid ass. He needed to take me to the doctor ASAP. I called him and explained how we needed to go to the clinic ASAP.

It was abortion time. I've lost count of how many abortions I've had being with this one man. Eye'z was explaining to me once again how he already had children, comparing his 5 to my 1, and how this was not good timing. While we're sitting in the abortion clinic waiting for my name to be called, I had a crazy feeling in my stomach: nervous and anxiety all over the place. Here he was talking bull.

The doctor explained to me that due to stress and the incident with catching Eye'z with the young lady and when I "fell down the stairs"—that's what I told the doctor, although I was really pushed down the stairs—one of my twin's had already passed away. Tears rolled down my face, and anger took over. How could I allow this to happen again? The doctor then explained to us how the second baby was living off his twin's oxygen. Once they removed the baby, he would pass away. It was a slim chance that the last baby would live (this was all due to a rare disease I have. Check it: I knew back then about my disease, but I paid no attention to what the doctors was telling me. Watch how it will catch up with me later. Just wait on it. Keep reading about "my life's journey.") God gives us signs and it's up to us to listen.

I knew at this point on "this walk of life," I couldn't allow Eye'z to continue to hurt me, nor did my body deserve to keep being abused. We both began to go in different directions, especially when I found out that the young lady had permanently moved to Chicago. I decided to enroll back into school for something quick in the medical field. Once I finished, I would work temporarily until the temp agency placed me with a permanent company. I just knew I had to change things in my life for my health, my daughter and well-being of my life. Stripping wasn't it. Plus, I needed long-term goals for my daughter. I felt like I was making all of the right choices.

Now I had to move on with my life. I gave up my car, and the apartment I found wasn't the best place. It was a start-over "New Jack City," but I called it our new home. The building looked exactly like the movie. I wanted a change where no one knew where I lived—especially Eye'z.

It felt great to be free from mess and sleeping with someone that didn't LOVE, RESPECT, or VALUE ME.

CHAPTER FOUR: Detour

My new chapter now begins: I have a new start. I've finished with school, and things are going extremely well. I have a temporary job in the medical field in Oakbrook. Waking up at the crack of dawn to catch two buses and two trains just to arrive to work at 8 a.m. has been a drain. Getting a new car ASAP was primary on my list. I've gotten my body back into shape with a little night "stripping" out West only on weekends whenever my baby girl was gone. I know I said I would stop; it's just for a second until I get my car. Then I was done for real.

Money was looking great, although it still wasn't enough to get my car, plus working the salaried job. When I was going to work, I started seeing a strange man in a silver-colored car with rims—a Lexus—same time every morning. He would pull up and ask me if I needed a ride. He had a chocolate complexion. This particular morning, it was freezing cold and I was dog-tired. So, when he asked me if I needed a ride, I said "Yes," and I got in the car. Mr. Stranger offered to buy me a car if I could bring his fantasy to life. I didn't know his name and I didn't care. Was this safe? NO.

But I needed the car. I know it was crazy stupid—
heck, this man could have killed me. I didn't think
nothing less of his "fantasy": he had me tie him
up, piss on him, apply hot wax, and I even used a
whip. I didn't have a clue as to what I was doing. I
had never experienced anything like this before.
Once I was finished, he told me to expect the car
in "2 days"—just off of someone's crazy fantasy.
Guess what? In two days, I had a car. And I
never saw him again—STRANGE!

Life was really looking up for me: my job had
offered me a full-time position with the company
after working for two months. Plus, I got a brand-
new car—despite its origin. Yes, things were
looking great for my new year. No more
"stripping," or crazy acts with strangers. I had
been so focused. I haven't even noticed that I
wasn't getting any cock. Next on my agenda was
to save a little bit more and move out of "New
Jack City." Soon, my daughter and I could say

"Goodbye" to the roaches, rats, prostitutes, and drug dealers. It was all becoming too dangerous living like this.

Seasons have changed and now, summer has arrived. My daughter was away with her dad, and I had been working extremely hard. It was time to get out and have some fun and reconnect with my siblings from my stepdad's side of the family. Hanging out on the porch, drinking, listening to music, playing cards and just having a good time with my people, the summer was just beginning.

Sitting on the porch talking mess, out steps this tall caramel delight just how I like them. I'll refer to him as "Youngster." My dreams just came to reality: his smile and crispy white linen shirt was fresh—and he smelled so good. I was so focused on his confident swag, wondering about the size of his manhood (was it super big?), that I was taken completely aback that so many knew him as he approached the porch. Everyone was speaking to him, shaking his hand, and giving him hugs. Who in the Sam hell is this man? My family introduced us, and I couldn't speak because my words got stuck. He just smiled at me; I blinked my eyes and instantly, my panties were soaking wet. I immediately went to the bathroom—I couldn't believe this right here. I should just throw him my panties right now and call it a night. Then I heard my name being called: "Hey Kesha, we're about to hit up a bar. Do you feel up to it?"

Of course, I wanted to go. I got myself together, got into my car, and met them at the bar. The night was still fresh. I wouldn't mind hearing some music and dancing the night out. As I'm dancing, I could feel his eyes all over my body, watching me as he was drinking. Me being who I am, gave him something to watch— "stripper" mode. I'm watching him watch me as I slowly walked towards him as he was licking his lips. I got closer to him and began to dance on him as he was sitting down. I could tell he wanted to touch me. Instead, I pushed his hands away and he smiled. It was like no one was at the bar but us two.

The music stopped, and the DJ played another song. I sat on his lap, so we could talk, and I could hear him. Feeling the warmth of his lips on my neck was making me warm inside, and of course, my panties wet. I couldn't tell you what our conversation was about: all I remember was hearing my brothers and cousins say, "You two good? We're heading out." I told them we were good. Then I took him to his car. "Can you go home with me?" I whispered in his ear. I wanted him to just have his way with me. Youngster said "Yes," with a smile and without hesitation. We left the bar headed straight to my apartment. We couldn't get in the door fast enough before he started to undress me kissing my nipples and taking my clothes off. He lifted me up and took me straight into my bedroom, laid me across the bed, took his shirt off and took me to sexual paradise.

Spreading my legs widely, his tongue was so long, wet, and the in-and-out motion was unbelievable. I had never been tasted like this before. My pussy was super wet, cummin', cummin' like water—just imagine we haven't fucked at all. Youngster was having the pleasure of eating my primed kitty. Then, he stopped, stood up keeping his eyes locked on mine the entire time while my heart was pounding. *Please don't be a disappointment.* My goodness, this man took his pants off, and his manhood started showing out through the imprint of his underwear, letting me know that it was long, hard, and thick. I couldn't wait any longer—I got on my knees, took my "prize" out—pulling, pulling, pulling—dang, this Long John was long! As I began to get in position, he pulled me up, bent me over, and took me to straight ecstasy. When I tell you, this escapade dick was worth the one-year wait. Every bit of it.

It's morning. I have to get Youngster the hell out of my place to his car without my siblings knowing that their older sister was an undercover slut. Youngster wasn't finished with me just yet. He rolled over to kiss my inner thigh, and instantly, I got moist all over again. Our morning felt like déjà vu from the night before. The morning turned into the afternoon, where we laid up in bed with lunch, conversation, and more sexual pleasure, which then lead into the late evening. This was definitely a way to get to know one another.

I started off my summer with my motto: "No feelings, no attachments." I didn't expect to have a deep, intimate relationship with Youngster. He was too young. I had exactly two months of summer to gain sexual pleasure from at least three more men with "no feelings, no attachments." Although I had my motto, Youngster was making himself real comfortable at my place, and I wasn't sure that I really liked the idea. My motto went straight out the back door. Youngster was spending more nights at my place, cooking; leaving bags of money in my dresser drawer; shopping; giving me flowers, and even taking me to expensive restaurants.

What I didn't like about Youngster disrupting my life was the missing in action for days at a time or even weeks. All of a sudden, he'd attempt to make up for his absence by giving me flowers, love notes on the bathroom mirror, or leave bags of money in my dresser drawer. At this point, I already knew that he wasn't "The One."

My summer was still fresh. I needed to focus on moving—not dealing with all of his shenanigans. I found a place that I didn't tell anyone about except for my good friend. Of course, Youngster was MIA again, so he didn't have a clue that I was moving. He didn't know my next move—not even my family knew. I felt like Youngster's sister, someone I partied with a lot, knew where he was located. He probably was at his "baby mother's house." Either way, I was moving on and she could deal with his things, or else they would be thrown away or sitting on the floor of the apartment. "No feelings, no attachments."

Moving day: "Goodbye New Jack City" and "Hello South Shore Drive." My good friend helped me move since she was the only one, I really trusted to know the location. We moved as fast as we could before Youngster decided to pop up. We must have packed our cars for at least three trips before we were done moving.

I felt like I could breathe again. New place. New attitude. New position. Life was definitely on the uptick, although old habits were hard to release. I began to hang back out with friends that I hadn't seen since my transition of moving. I was no longer embarrassed of where I lived. Once you're in your comfort zone, sometimes you go back to the "norm" without realizing that the "norm" wasn't the best decision. It's just a familiar place.

I was really enjoying my new place. Work kept me extremely busy from hanging out with my friends, and I still needed to get my daughter from her dad's house since school was soon starting. Besides, I knew she was going to enjoy her bedroom, and I wanted to desperately spend quality time with her. Lately, I have been extremely tired. I just did not have enough energy. I'm so glad I had a stable job with insurance so I could start attending to my health.

Summer was fun while it lasted, and now it was time to say hello to fall. My baby girl arrived home before the start of school. We were still adjusting to our new place and enjoying each other's company. It was so precious to be living in a place of peace, with no hallway fighting, arguing neighbors, drug deals gone wrong, or gunshots late at night. But seriously, this throwing–up, having no energy, and feeling faint was catching up with me. I had to hurry up and make an appointment. Until then, I also had to plan my party for my birthday.

October would be here in no time, and I wanted

all my family to show up. My cousin, my baby sister, and I were celebrating our birthdays' together. Oh yes, and of course, my exe's were invited—Eye'z and Youngster. Call me petty or messy—who cared— they could come and see my progress. I hadn't seen either of them since I moved away without telling them. They still talked to my brothers, so they knew the tea.

I couldn't wait to see my good girlfriend. We talked every night on the phone. Things were looking up for Michelle: new job, new car, and from what she'd been telling me, there were some fine men at her job too. They had been hanging out and she was going to invite a few to my party. "I can't wait," I excitedly told her. I was about to have a good ole time.

It's my birthday—tonight was the party. I'm looking sexy as hell: my hair was done, and my outfit was just right. My check list was complete. Headed to the hood right off 55th and Ashland Street, this little hole in the wall bar was always jumping. Music, drinks—everything was going good so far. Everybody's having a good time, and I'm dancing the night away as if my exe's weren't even there.

Michelle walked in with her coworkers.
Immediately, I couldn't help but notice one man in
particular. He was of medium height and build,
and he was a well-dressed man. I like a good-
looking man when I see one. And I know what I
want when I see it. Some might say I'm a whore
while others might say I liked to have fun.
Michelle came over and introduced me to the
gentlemen. One named Aaron caught my full
attention. Right away, he asked what I was
drinking and if the birthday girl liked to dance. I
couldn't say no to my guest—it was something
about him that mesmerized me. It was like I didn't
know anyone else was at the party. The music
was to our beat and I tuned everyone out. The
way his body moved with mine on the dance floor
was amazing. My dance with Eye'z couldn't
compare. Aaron was seductive. He moved with
me in sync as if we knew each other for a long
time. This man had me under a spell. In the next
minute, the party was broken up. Police were
yelling everyone had to go. The bar was closing.
My family was screaming about some punks who
had just robbed Eye'z and my brothers' face-

down on the ground at gunpoint.

It was time to go, but before leaving, I had to first exchange numbers with Aaron. We had to finish what we started…and it definitely wasn't talking. Have you ever heard the saying, "People know who they're going to sleep with the first time they see someone?" Well, I knew each and every time I saw a man I wanted to conquer in the bed. The saying wasn't a cliché. It was the truth.
Michelle called me the next day to give me the "tea" about Aaron. Everything I heard, I liked. She went on to tell me how they were going to a coworker's party on the weekend. "Let me work on a babysitter, and I'll get back with you." Boom: it's the weekend and I've got my babysitter on lock! I haven't talked to Aaron. He hasn't called me, nor have I called him. I didn't want to seem thirsty. I told Michelle we should go somewhere else, but she insisted we drop by for a minute then leave and meet up with some more friends afterwards. As we were pulling up to the party, guess who was the first person I saw when we walked into the door? Aaron. He saw me and instantly stopped talking to a young lady near him, grabbed my arm and took me straight to the

dance floor.

My girl Michelle didn't even get a chance to introduce me to anyone else. Aaron was so thirsty to get me to the dance floor so we could finish where we left off. I couldn't believe his behavior was turning me on. As the music was playing and our bodies began to move, he caught me back up into his seductiveness. When he placed his lips on my neck, I began to melt. He whispered into my ear and I started to get moist. It was like I was stuck in his arms. I could feel him growing. It was as if we were on the dance floor making mad erotic pleasure. This man definitely had some kind of spell because he had my sweet kitty throbbing. As the music stopped, he whispered in my ear, "I'm going home with you." I couldn't resist. I had to have him as much as he had to have me. I went over to Michelle and told her I was leaving with Aaron and I would tell her more later—she wasn't mad. Instead, she smiled, told me she'd call me, and to enjoy my night. That's the kind of friendship we had. Michelle understood me and I her. Meeting Aaron meant that he was about to introduce me to a different sexual world I had never encountered. Was I ready?

In the car, we shared small talk just trying to get to know a few things about each other. We even laughed about sexual positions! Once we arrived at my place, I directed him straight to my bedroom. Gently, he laid me onto the bed. He wasn't rushing. Slowly, he removed each piece of my clothing, watching my everybody movement. Towered over me to kiss my belly button, I inhaled as he took his time kissing down my stomach, slowly spreading my legs. Breathing heavily, I watched him take his time. His lips were so warm, wet and juicy. Sighing with my eyes closed, he began to taste my sweetly scented passionflower. I was running like a faucet. He worked his way back up to my breasts, and slowly placed his fingers inside of me. I was getting wetter as he then slowly entered me. Our motion was similar to when we were dancing at the bar. The sex was dynamic. We finished, and Aaron explained how he hated to leave, but he had to get home. He told me that he'd call me later in the week.

Immediately, I called Michelle, and gave her every juicy detail after detail. We laughed and went over the girl code: "Don't call him, let him call you." She said he'd want more. The code worked: Aaron called me, and I was ecstatic. We had an interesting conversation: he kept asking me strange questions about women, like if I had ever been with a woman? Would I mind being with a woman? Have I ever had a threesome? How did I become so great in giving head jobs? I'm thinking to myself, "*What kind of mess have I gotten myself into "NOW"?*" As I explained to him, even during my stripping days, I was never exposed to those things except for dancing for a woman, but never anything sexual.

Aaron smoothly said, "Well, let me be the first to help you explore that curiosity inside of you with me and my woman."

"Woman?" Wait a minute. I thought he was single. I guess we never got a chance to talk about that, huh! I was being too much like a man thinking with my pussy and not my brain. Pointedly, I asked, "Well, does your lady approve of you having sex with other women?"

"We have an open relationship. I'm able to test a woman out, and if I get a good feeling about her, I'll bring the woman to our bedroom, introduce her to my lady. But she has to be worth bringing her to our bedroom." OMG. *What kind of shit have I gotten myself into?*

I'm a risk taker, and I've always been a curious person when it came to my sexuality. A few months went by and eventually, I broke down and piqued my sexual threesome interest. When I started back talking to Aaron, we spent a lot of time on the telephone having phone sex, or we were meeting up to have sex. Then it was time for my first rendezvous. It was a weekday evening, and we were on the telephone having phone sex. All of a sudden, I heard a female's voice asking him if he needed help. Invitingly, he says, "Yea, join in on the call." I froze up. What should I do: hang up or keep going? In a silky voice, Aaron's woman, Ericka, says, "Don't be afraid Kesha. Keep on going and I'll help you." I keep talking, and then he commands Ericka to suck his dick. "Keisha's a good girl when she sucks my dick."

Aaron told me to keep talking. The more I talked, I realized it was actually turning me on. His woman then told him to tell me to play with myself. I closed my eyes and began to imagine her sucking my pussy. As she's giving him head, I'm moaning, he's moaning, she's moaning. Next thing you know, I heard her jerking him off. I'm getting hotter with each jerk. All of a sudden, I asked him to cum in her mouth. "Is that what you want?" I told him yes. He screamed, "I'm cummin'! I say I'm cummin'!"

That's the first time I had experienced "phone threesome sex". I didn't ever plan on telling my friend Michelle although I needed to tell someone. If I couldn't talk about it, I'd write about it. So, I began keeping journals of my life. After the phone sex experience with Aaron and Ericka, we eventually had our first threesome date night set. Now I was questioning: am I bi-sexual? How would I know? I couldn't ask anyone—not even my good girlfriend Michelle. She had been extremely busy hanging out with Aaron's best friend. I wondered if they were alike. I would never know. I'd never tell her what I'd been doing. And I'm pretty sure Michelle wouldn't tell me either.

Aaron set everything up for our first date night at a bar out South. I arrived with Aaron, nervous as ever. He told me to relax, and that I'd been doing great over the phone. Seeing that I needed to calm down, Aaron bought me a drink. My nerves were everywhere. One because of this date. Plus, I didn't do any of my sexual dirt out South; everything I did was out West. Aaron nudged me, "She's here." I instantly saw Ericka walking towards us. Confidence showed in her walk, and her skin was a beautiful mocha complexion. Her figure was like a Coca-Cola bottle with all of the right proportions: big butt, small wrists, plump breasts, and short in stature. I smiled at her. Aaron introduced us and he gave her a kiss. She leaned over and kissed me. I couldn't believe I didn't move or push her away. I leaned over and kissed her back. We didn't care if anyone was watching.

Aaron was THE MAN this date night. He kept the drinks flowing. We laughed, talked, and danced all night long. Guess what? After the date, Aaron took me home.

On Wednesday I received a call very late at night: "Get dressed and meet us out West at this club." I knew exactly where they were. I did exactly as I was told. I put on something so little, that it wouldn't be hard to take off. This was it—the night I was about to have my first experience. I pulled up to the club; there weren't a lot of people in the place. I saw Aaron and his girlfriend sitting in a booth waiting on me. Before I could say anything, he told me to dance. I took my coat off and I began to dance for her. Ericka sat there intently watching me. I could feel Aaron's eyes all over my body. The heat was turning up in this booth; I got closer to her: she's touching my body, and Aaron was just watching us as we interacted with one another. I could see him out of the corner of my eyes as he pulled his cock out, playing with himself. His girlfriend then caressed my breasts, as we began to kiss. She put her lips on my breasts as I'm watching her tongue go around my nipples, sucking on my breasts. I turned towards Aaron and I began to suck his dick. Ericka's watching me, playing with herself with her fingers. Aaron gestured for her to join us. She pulled up a chair, and I sat on her lap. She's playing with my pussy as I'm sucking his dick. Suddenly, Aaron began to cum all in my mouth—right there in the club. YES—everything went on in this place and nobody saw anything.

It's weird that I received a telephone call on a night I knew Aaron wasn't with his girlfriend. It's getting more and more sexual between the two of us. Ericka was on the line and she wanted me to come over to talk. I didn't know what to think—was she about to end our sexual relationship? I headed over, walked into the house and saw that the lights were dimmed, and music was playing. Ericka welcomed me by handing me a drink. She then told me to put on a laced-up nightgown with no panties. "Where's Aaron?"

"We have an open relationship and I'm allowed to play without him."

"Hmm" sounds familiar, right? She grabbed my hand, leading me towards their bedroom. Candles were lit everywhere. This would be my first encounter with just a woman. In a sultry voice, Ericka said, "Just relax and enjoy yourself." We laid down in the bed. She began to oil my body down and gave me a massage. Every motion was soft and with passion. We began to kiss each other, then she started to suck my breasts, leading down my belly button into my pussy. Her head job was better than Aarons; it was as if she knew my body. She whispered, "I wanted you to taste me just like you taste Aaron." I did as she asked me. We took our time. The next thing blew my mind: Ericka put on a strap-on-dildo. I had never seen or did anything like this in my life. I just relaxed and enjoyed the rest of the night. We were good and ready for round two when Aaron came home from work. When he arrived home, he took a shower and we joined him. We then gave him the best night... It was like I was in a relationship with a man and a woman.

Strangely, the conversation totally switched up as we were all lying in bed together. She propositioned me with what seemed to be an out of the world question: "Have you ever thought about getting paid to have sex with couples?" " No, I never thought about it...but, I'm open to the proposition." It seemed like the more time I spent around Aaron and his girlfriend, the more I was falling down a dark hole with more entanglements. First, Aaron showed me the lifestyle of having a threesome. Now, his girlfriend Ericka wanted to introduce me to other couples.

I knew it was so far-fetched, but it was like I was already in the dark hole. I might as well go a little deeper. I accepted the offer and was compensated very well. My role was to go into a couple's bedroom, demonstrate for the woman how to give great fellatio and teach the man how to seduce his woman. The job didn't last long—maybe a year. I was getting bored, or maybe my real feelings were that all of this was just too much. Too strange. I could feel something was pulling on me. Another crazy thing happened: I had to end the relationship with Aaron and his girlfriend Ericka. It was doing something to me like an "attachment." I knew this type of lifestyle wasn't right. Sleeping with both of them or other couples in general was not the plan for my life.

I'm not gonna lie: it was hard moving forward with my life. No late-night calls or phone sex. Deep down inside, I knew better. Initially, I thought it was fun exploring and experimenting. But these things can't last forever. And my life couldn't be set-up like this while raising my daughter. I didn't want her to think that being in these types of entanglements was the way you lived. Nor did I want my family to know that type person lived inside of me, although I kept so many secrets from my family. The secrets were destroying me. It was like I was living another life—God couldn't be pleased with my behavior.

New Changes in My Life Again...

I was getting blessed with another new position. This was a great move for me with the company, working in the city closer to my daughter's school. On top of that, my hours weren't long, and I no longer had to drive all the way out to the suburbs. Sometimes when you think something's too good to be true, you need to believe it and run the other direction.

Working at this new clinic site was a miserable mistake. The repetition of the job bored me, and I was constantly sick. I didn't know if the women in here were making me sick, with their old messy behavior (except for two women whom I grew to care for), or coming to the same place doing the same old boring things day in and day out was negatively affecting me. Maybe what's wrong with me was that I hadn't gone to get a check-up like I had planned a long time ago. I kept putting it off, saying that I'd get to it but "not yet." Too late. No more waiting.

Welp, I was at work when I passed out on the work-site floor. This isn't what I needed right now: being off work at anybody's hospital, with no one to care for my daughter "financially." I found out that I had ovarian cancer and I had to have an immediate hysterectomy and blood transfusions. All of this was discovered at the most inconvenient time when I'd just started this new position!

This can't be happening right now. What am I going to do? I didn't have any insurance. But I couldn't think about that. My first priority was to get back to Oakbrook, IL. I needed more money and I missed working with people who cared about me. Then I could focus on getting insurance in October.

I had been off work for a few days now. I wasn't

ready to go back to work, but I didn't see any other option for me. Who else was going to take care of me and my daughter? So back to the clinic from hell. Piles of work were stacked on my desk giving me an instant headache. These messy old women acted like they cared, asking about my welfare when all they were really doing was being nosy. The only two people who genuinely cared were Karen and Renee. When Karen saw me, she told me that someone had been asking about me. It was a young man that came into the clinic daily to pick up the urine samples and blood. Karen's smiling as she says to me "I believe he's single and I know he's a good guy. I know you're single and you need help with your daughter." I knew exactly what gentleman she was talking about. I paid him attention, but not really because I thought he was taken. He was so fine with honey-dipped skin, a tall frame with a well-built body. Why would he care about my well-being? Why would he even notice me? I'm not exactly the prettiest but I can hold my own. Evidently, something about me caught his attention for him to be watching me and for him and Karen to have been talking about me. "Well, what's his name?" Instead of replying,

Karen laughed.

"I'll let you guys talk when he comes in to pick up the samples today." I shrugged my shoulders and smiled. As I'm making the shoulder gesture, guess who walked right in? Looking somewhat shy, I said, "Good afternoon." Looking directly in my face, he smiled with such a bright grin that felt so full of life. I'd never paid attention to his smile before. "Hello young lady. How are you feeling?" "Better." Wow, he noticed I was gone too. His concern made me feel warm inside.

"You was missed." He kept his eyes steady on me.
"Who me?" Laughing, he smiled, then he walked away to retrieve the urine and blood. He rarely talked—maybe that's why I never thought he would pay me attention. As he was leaving, I got up the nerve to ask his name. "Excuse me, what's your name?"
"Ralph. And yours?"
"Kesha," I smiled at him as he said "I'll see you tomorrow. Make sure you take care of yourself now." Ralph and I shared a smile as he headed towards the clinic exit.

"I will. Now I have a reason to come to work tomorrow."

Looking forward to work every day, Ralph and I spoke to each other regularly at the clinic. We then exchanged telephone numbers and talked every day. He was a great friend, listener and encourager. We had been talking about hooking up just to go out. Nothing's happened between us just yet. I enjoyed his company. Ralph was like a male version of a best friend that I never had. He was concerned about my health and wanted me to get my surgery. I had been applying for other jobs and looking for apartments. With his support, I scheduled my surgery. Within the company, I applied for a position back in the Oakbrook, IL location.

I secured the job in the same department with a different position, paying much more money with insurance. Before I moved into my new position, my surgery was scheduled, and I was slated to be off work for 8-10 weeks. Living on South Shore Drive was nice, but the rent was just too expensive for my life right now. A cheaper apartment in Englewood would keep my daughter and I sheltered, and it was affordable.

Surgery day was scary. Just the thought of my womanhood about to be taken away, was hard to comprehend. On the bright side, there would be no more cancer. My mother, friends, and family were all with me or called to find out details and the progress of the surgery. When I woke up, I was startled to see my mother at the bottom of my bed praying at my feet. I heard stories about me not waking up during the expected time. The recovery time was supposed to have been only three hours after surgery then I was supposed to wake up. But I didn't wake up for another eight hours after I was taken to my room. The doctors said the surgery was a success and there were no more signs of the tumors. I was the youngest person to have this kind of surgery procedure done. Life for me was changing again.

God gave me another chance. Now what will I do with it: get saved? I had a lot of time to think during recovery. I wrote in my journal on a regular basis; I changed my circle of friends; and most importantly, I built a closer relationship with God. I also had a friend who became my best friend. In my old life, we would've made fun of her for "being a Christian." We would have judged her because she was so religious. She chose not to party like us because she had responsibilities as a parent and provider for her home. She was the one who God used to bring me into the church house. I was raised in church although as an adult I wasn't active and didn't attend as much. Church was more like a revolving door, where I entered and left whenever I felt a serious need from God. I would get afraid when people walked up to me at church and spoke over my life. Instead of embracing God's truth about my life, I ran to my comfort zone: the streets.

My life was definitely headed in a positive direction. Everything was looking good. I was attending church on a regular basis. I attended bible study and was active on the New Members ministry. I had a steady job, a safe home, a reliable car, my daughter was happy, and I was in good health. What detour could happen at this point? I was not expecting any—except when I met Mr. Charming.

A very good friend of many years passed away, so I went to his funeral. Mr. Charming was at the funeral as well. His smile got me—not his looks. The first thing we did was give one another a hug; it was just a tragedy how our friend passed away. It seemed like that hug was a bitter and invisible entanglement that I really was not prepared for at this time in my life. After the funeral, Mr. Charming and I started getting to know each other. We would text every day. I wasn't sexually attracted to him. What I did like was his concern for my well-being. He cared about my laughter, and my family and friends knew him. He was very interested in the new church I had just joined. He'd attend service with me if he were in town since he mainly worked on the road. I wasn't looking for anything long-term with him. I couldn't explain our relationship. I really wanted to be with Ralph. I believe I was passing time with Mr. Charming and I should've let his butt pass me straight by. It seemed like I'd fall into a pattern with men, falling for those that gave me attention or knew when to step in, especially if I was in a vulnerable and desperate stage in my life.

There were signs I had ignored about Mr. Charming. Whenever he was home from off the road, he would always stop by with gifts, and spend many nights at my place. I was barely going out with my girlfriends anymore. I was still always at church. He knew where I was, or I'd wait on a call from him letting me know when he was on his way home, so I could meet him at his house. Weekends were great with him. We would have date nights, dinner dates, or stay at his house and watch movies.

Mr. Charming was a lady's man, and he was cool with the fellas, but there was just something a little odd about him. After I got saved, I stopped drinking and cursing. Mr. Charming would encourage me to keep up the good work. But there was something really off with him. Things began to change with Mr. Charming. One evening, I remember him surfing the internet on the computer. When he was home, he'd catch up on his emails, social media, and surf whatever else online. Well, this one evening I looked up and asked him a question. I had startled him. "Who are you talking to?" He had such a weird look in his eyes. Hurriedly, he logged off the computer mumbling "No one."

"Well, are you going to come to bed?" He laid down—but something still didn't feel right about Mr. Charming. The next day, I went home. He told me he would call me while he was heading back on the road. Puzzled, I said, "It's Saturday."

Looking unprepared, "Oh yeah, they wanted me to make some extra money." This was strange; he never wanted to make extra money before. I didn't contest. Later, I called Mr. Charming. He wasn't answering my calls, or my texts. Something was fishy—his patterns were changing. Sunday came and no Mr. Charming. In an investigative mood, he failed to realize I knew where he parked on Sundays. After service, I drove to his exact parking spot. Surprise, surprise, his vehicle was there. I politely texted him and explained that he was a liar and that he was still home: he was just at someone else's home.

Once the weekend was over, Mr. Charming was calling, texting sorry apologies. What do I do? Accept his sad apologies with a gifted pair of boots. The next weekend came up and it's quite peculiar. Maybe it's the fall leaves, the cold, or the rain... All I knew was that Mr. Charming was acting funny. We had set a date to go to the movies. The arrangements were as usual: I told him the time of the show, and then I'd meet him at his house, park my car, and then we would ride together like normal. However, when I got to the house, I felt funny. I got out of the car and approached his house and rang the bell. Mr. Charming opened the door, but he's not dressed. "Is everything alright?" He went to his room and sat at the computer desk while I stood at his door. He had that same look in his eyes again that I saw the last week. Irritated, Mr. Charming says, "Stop asking me questions." I didn't think much about his comment and I asked again, "What's wrong? Do you want to go to the show? Why aren't you dressed?"

Question after question, his face got more twisted and angrily contorted. He was definitely agitated. All of a sudden, Mr. Charming started yelling at me. His voice sounded like it was booming through the walls. Calmly, I said "I'm just asking you a few questions. I could've stayed at home."

He jumped up and his female roommate—

another ignored red flag—closed her bedroom door. Turning and looking back, I said, "What's that all about?"

"STOP FUCKING ASKING ME ALL THESE QUESTIONS," Mr. Charming angrily belted out. I chuckled. "What's so fucking funny?" All of a sudden, complete rage replaced any "charm" Mr. Charming may have ever displayed. In one swift move, he grabbed me off my feet, and took me straight into the hallway. He lifted me up off the floor, with my feet dangling. I couldn't breathe. Looking into his eyes, all I could see was red fire. Wait. I needed oxygen. I was coughing, choking. "Mr. Charming!" His roommate screamed his name. Suddenly, I fell. I was on the floor crawling to the kitchen. I was about to kill this bastard. I couldn't get there fast enough to get the knives, before I was thrown out of the house.

Hot tears ran down my face. I called my best friend and she calmed me down. She told me to meet her at the nearest police station. My hair on my skin was raised with goosebumps. I couldn't believe what had just happened. My tears made it hard for me to see while driving to the station. I was so glad to see her. She was right there for me when I needed her most. Once we got inside of the station, the police ran his name, address, and date of birth. I would have given his Social Security number too if I had it. An officer informed us that Mr. Charming's name was indeed in the database, and he was known for domestic violence in his previous relationship. A male officer asked me, "Did you know this?"

Frustrated, I responded, "Not at all." Before we left the station, the police immediately got into their cars and headed straight towards his house to arrest him. When we arrived, the roommate lied and told the police he didn't live there. With clenched fists, I yelled, "She's a liar! His vehicle was outside." The police then told me they couldn't do anything without a warrant. They informed me that I could head back to the station, fill a report out, and to appear in court. I filled out the report.

On the drive home I felt violated, disrespected—hot tears started streaming down my face again. My friend called to check on me, and I was grateful. All I could think about was *How could this happen? Why didn't I see this coming?* I hated to admit it, but I knew that I ignored the signs. What was I going to tell my family? He was supposed to be the family man and friend. He was Mr. Charming. This was just unbelievable. Weeks passed. I kept receiving phone calls. No one's saying anything. There's only breathing. Finally, the day of court the caller decided to say something. "I'm sorry. Why do we have to go to court? People won't believe you. That wasn't me. You're making things up in your mind…" All of the typical pathetic passive-aggressive tactics an abuser uses to blame the victim. Trying to shame us and make us feel like we're crazy, so that we don't do anything.

The phone call made me feel afraid. I didn't go to court. I thought he would catch me outside of the courthouse and hurt me again. I buried this domestic violence abuse for seven years from my memory. I truly thought I had forgotten about him, until one day someone I was talking to said "Do you remember Mr. Charming?" My skin was singed with all of the hurt, anger, and pain. It all began to resurface. I realized that I had not yet forgiven him.

Yet again, I was trying to get back on track...

CHAPTER FIVE: My Burning Desire

I'm back to talking to Ralph on a regular basis. Why not give us another try? This time, we will take it slow and get to know one another. Ralph was a great man. He was the right man for me. I just knew it in my heart, that we would go through the storm. Ralph had always been there for me in my darkest times: from depression, sickness, personal dilemma, Ralph has been consistent in my life.

After putting in a full day at work and driving a long commute back home, Ralph and I would mostly spend time together or plan to spend time over the weekends. He worked weekends, so we would try to work around one another's schedule, which made my LOVE grow for him every day. Our conversations over the telephone were better than anything, plus spending weekends together. The smallest things would make me happy; just spending time on his breaks brought great joy to me. The more we spent time talking over the telephone or visiting during his short lunch break visits, I wanted to be with him more.

It's the weekend and I'm getting ready to hang out. I was going to be out West—Ralph lived out West. I let him know that I was hanging out and he told me to be careful and to call him when I was finished. Maybe I could stop by. *I finally get to see where he stayed.* This is a big move in our relationship. Chewing my bottom lip, I tell him "Ralph, it's going to be late when I finish hanging out."

"That's alright," he says smoothly. "I'll be woke." The bar closed at 2 a.m. I called Ralph, and he immediately answered. "Hey, I'm leaving the bar now. Maybe I should wait until another night to come over..." *Don't agree with me. Tell me to come over.*

Coolly, I could tell he was smiling through the phone. "Ah nah, it's alright to come by. My address is 1816 W. Broadway. I'll stay on the phone with you until you get to my place."

I drove around for 30 minutes looking for a park. I was nervous as ever, and butterflies were fluttering all in my stomach. I've been waiting on this moment with him. Finally finding a park, Ralph met me outside. We walked to his apartment in excited silence. He leads me down the stairs to his place. Romantic candles are lit everywhere, and soft music was playing. No one has ever done anything like this before—this was just another way he showed me he really cared. I think I could be with this man forever.

As we're standing face-to-face, I looked up at his tall frame. We're breathing heavily. He began to kiss me so passionately. Pulling me closer, I feel his strong, yet gentle hands remove the straps of my dress one at a time. Slowly, my dress falls onto the floor. I'm standing in my underwear. Ralph is taking in all of me in admiration. I didn't feel strange or funny. Actually, I was quite turned how he was watching me and admiring my body. Taking my hand, he led me into his room. Still no words, I laid down on the bed while he planted soft kisses all over my body. His lips were so warm—starting at my neck, shoulder, breast, then my stomach—while the Isley Brothers softly played in the background. Inhaling deeply, he hits my spot. As he took his time, I closed my eyes and felt the passion. "Relax baby," he briskly whispers in my ear. I can't stand it: this man has made LOVE to me. This is how he becomes my heart and my desire.

I couldn't get enough of him. But it seemed like just as soon as we got close, distance was going to be the only thing in common between us. Days became weeks. Weeks became months. And months became wasted time waiting. Holidays would come and go. No time was spent with Ralph because he was always working. Then the telephone calls went from every day to once a week. All of a sudden, he didn't answer the telephone or any text messages. Ralph had so many catchy cliché phrases—LIES. He would say, "Keesh, it's just a cellphone. It's not attached to my hip at all times." No more lunch break stops. Just nothing. I began to feel lonely. Every time we spoke, we began arguing. I'm starting to rethink this relationship thing with him. How can you be lonely in a relationship? Well, when you feel as if you're putting more effort into it, that's how. Is this man my future? Am I the ying to his yang?

How did we end up here? I finally found out Ralph had been having family issues. Plus, his new start up business wasn't taking off like he had anticipated. It seemed as if he was drawing further away from me. I couldn't lose my best friend and my lover. He was always there for me when I went through my ups and downs. I didn't want to be selfish; I needed to be taken care of, and I had needs to feel wanted. Ralph was not giving me what I needed. I'm so sick of arguing about nothing. Now, when we saw each other, it was only sexual. Our conversations were so boring. I was constantly pressing the issue about seeing him, his children and family. Especially when I felt as if he knew all about me and my family. I felt like a stranger in this thing called a relationship. Only thing I knew was where he stayed, worked, and the vehicle he drove. I felt so naïve. I felt like I fell into another bad relationship. How does this keep happening to me?

It's time to redirect my life and stop focusing on someone that didn't care about me or didn't know the meaning of true LOVE. I decided to take a daycare class and step out on FAITH. I was beyond exhausted from working all the way out in Westchester: no promotion, constantly training individuals and not being recognized for all of my hard work—and my daughter needed me more than anything right now since she was pregnant with twins and she was experiencing complications.

I had a new church home where I enjoyed volunteering my time. It was time to start loving me. It felt great to be doing me and not focusing on a man. Of course, I hadn't heard from Ralph in over a month. When I finally spoke to him, he put all the blame on me. Wow, really? guess how the conversation starts Trying to pout, he started in blaming me. "You haven't called your man at all to check on me. I guess you don't care anymore. You don't LOVE me." I could barely keep my emotions in check from wanting to slap him in the head. I don't LOVE him?

There's that famous four-letter word that kept coming around. He continued with his "famous cliché phrases." See, Keesh, when I love people, it's a different kind of LOVE." *What type of bull is this to feed me?* How can someone they love allow days, or even weeks to go past? Clenching my fists, I spouted, "Ralph, just stop it with the games. I guess you realized the phone calls and texting had stopped. The phone worked both ways. My life has to move forward, I have a daughter that needs me and twins that are now in the hospital everyday fighting for their lives. If you really wanted to call me, you know how to call me too."

My strong moment only lasted just that—a moment. I fell for his okie-doke lies and accepted the apology right along with the excuses that "this wouldn't happen again." He was here for us now that his sister had moved out. He would be a better man. I was not going to allow Ralph's lies to stop me from doing what I had started. I'd noticed the more I didn't pay him any attention, the more he was right there, back picking up calls, visiting one another over the weekends and even taking me out on dates. I just couldn't let him go: the sexual pleasure was just too good.

I was now back on track with getting my daycare business ready to kick off. I left my job, stepping out on faith. I was putting ads out for daycare services, and I was getting ready for one of the twins to come home from the hospital. Being able to help my daughter with going to college, I was at home full-time as the babies' provider/grandma and to fulfill my dreams as a business owner. Ralph did indeed step up when I decided to leave my job. He was there to help me out.

Ralph was a peculiar man. He truly did show his love differently. This is why I couldn't see us not being without one another. But I was starting to feel as if we were slipping apart. I never seemed to understand the purpose behind our "relationship." How could someone be with an individual for so many years and have this yearning, desire and fire that burned in my heart for him? Why did it feel like I was trapped in a world of emotional manipulation? People assume it's so easy to walk away. I couldn't understand it for the life of me; it was so hard to leave him alone.

"Emotional manipulation is a form of abuse where it involves the feeling or pressure to act a certain way because you're afraid of certain consequences or that a person will stop loving them. It can be very destructive to the victim's mental health. It is a big RED flag that a relationship isn't healthy. They are toxic to one another."

Another holiday has come, and I have found myself lonely once again. Now in the beginning of our relationship I would receive "make-up time gifts" or late gifts that we would buy for one another.

It still wasn't enough for me. It hurt in the past and honestly, it still hurts to think about everything: when you don't even receive a phone call. Broken promises after promises. It would be painful to hear from Ralph the next day just to hear him say, "Oh, I was working, then I went home and went to sleep." I would always say love shouldn't hurt, and Ralph would ask how did I know how L.O.V.E felt. GOD loved us and it didn't hurt. Your heart doesn't feel like broken pieces, wounded and scarred. Ralph didn't care. He only did what I allowed him to do. As holidays passed me by, it became year after year, and I began to become numb towards Ralph's absence not being there on holidays, I stopped asking, pleading with him. My heart couldn't handle the crying and pain anymore. Just imagine New Year's Eve approaching…how I would hate to see the New Year. Not bringing in the New Year with the one you would like to spend your life with. I kept staying with Ralph because I knew that it was going to take me a minute to hurt him just as much as he hurt me. Karma was real.

Things were looking up for me again. Business was slow, but I met another group of friends at church and a new friend in the daycare business. Ralph was beginning to notice change in me. I was done wasting my time. Don't get me wrong: I loved him. It just was not enough to stay. I occupied my time by helping my new friend Samantha with getting her daycare business together as she also opened up a beauty salon. Rehearsal with the dance ministry, volunteering with the outreach at church, caring for the twins and my daughter also added to my plate to keep me busy. I was still missing a piece of my life being in a relationship with Ralph, not getting the attention that I needed. No matter what I did, he acted as if he didn't notice what I was doing. How much confidence he had in me when I said I was at home or any other place I told him. This thing that we had going on was ridiculous and unacceptable.

My new girlfriend Samantha had opened up a beauty salon and it was nice. It still needed a little work, but I was so proud of her. Yes, honey, she did that—daycare and beauty salon owner. If we weren't working our daycare businesses after hours, we were hanging out at the shop. Samantha kept talking about a certain guy who was her best friend that would also have her back. I thought for a second that she was trippin' because this "friend" never seemed to come around. The only best friend that I'd met of hers was a female. But ok, I'd go with the flow. The more she spoke of him, the more he sounded like he was a good person.

It was a cool October night, and me and Samantha happened to have been coming back from dinner and we rode past the shop. It looked lit up. Samantha wanted to make a quick stop and she asked me to stay in the car, while she ran in to see what was going on. When she returned back to the car, she wasn't alone. A mocha-complexioned short guy was standing next to her. He looked cocky, full of personality, with a drink in his hand. Samantha introduced us. "Kesha, this is Isaiah—my best friend I've been telling you about." We both say hello. Then he said something kinda slick under his breath. I couldn't remember, but I thought to myself *Oh, I see he's a jokester*, although I didn't find anything funny. I just smiled. They stood around talking, making jokes, then he gave her a hug and asked us what we were about to get into. I just looked at him as Samantha replied, "Oh, Kesha's about to take me home."

Throwing a bottle away in the trash, Isaiah said "Ok. You ladies have a great evening, and it was nice meeting you Kesha."

Smiling politely, I replied. "It was nice meeting you too." I didn't think anything else about that night.

The more I began to hang out at the beauty shop with Samantha on Friday or Saturday nights, the more I began to see Isaiah. In my opinion, he was such an asshole. I couldn't stand him. He was "Mr. Know-it all" and "Mr. Cocky." Short men think they stand on top of the world; I guess it's a height thing where they feel they have to prove something to the world. It's now November and I wanted to do something for Samantha's birthday since she was always helping me out. I made the plans that my best friend and I were going to take her out for Mexican food and a few of her friends— namely Isaiah—was invited. I didn't want him to come, but since it was about Samantha and not me, why not? All of their birthdays were in November.

Why didn't I get a red flag about this man either? He was a wolf dressed in sheep's clothing. Isaiah pulled up outside, and I sat in the front seat since I knew where we were going. As we're driving, the conversation was going very well. He's talking with sense and there was not a drink in his hands. Sitting in the restaurant, all of Samantha's friends weren't able to join us, so it was just the four of us, which worked out well. We're laughing, joking and come to find out, Isaiah didn't care for me either.

He thought I was stuck-up, since every time he saw me, I was turning up my nose. Our night ended up at the adult sex toy store. We looked around at some of the dildos, and other products. Then it was time to go home. I told Isaiah that I truly enjoyed his conversation, and it was great getting to know him. Isaiah and Samantha dropped me and my best friend back at my house. Before she left, she said, "I believe Mr. Isaiah likes you and you feel the same."

Laughing, I told her he wasn't my type and that I was happy with Ralph— A few days had passed, and I headed over to Samantha's house, just to hang out since my daycare closed at 6 p.m. All my kids were gone, and my daughter was at home with the twins. Once I arrived at her house, guess who opened the door? Isaiah. "What a surprise," I smiled at him.

"Yeah, I've been over here helping out for a minute until I got a new job." He opened the door wider to let me enter the house.

"That's cool." I may be wrong about Mr. Cocky. We're talking and making fun of each other, just relaxing. Samantha wasn't able to leave, so I offered to take Isaiah home, since it was getting late and he was ready to go home. This gave me a great opportunity to get more information about him, ask where he has been, and just to be nosy digging around more into his life. My sudden interest seemed like it came out of nowhere.

What a ride home. The conversation was great. It's just like he opened up to me and we flowed. He told me so much about where he was from; what he had been going through; and he even told me about being shot. We sat outside of his house for hours talking all night getting to know one another and laughing. The next thing I knew, it was 4 a.m. in the morning. I had to get home. I had to open the daycare at 6 a.m. Well, looka there: he's not an asshole after all.

CHAPTER SIX: The mask

I haven't been thinking about Ralph since I had been hanging out with Samantha and Isaiah. We hung out throughout the week and even on the weekends. I was enjoying conversations with Isaiah. It was refreshing getting to know someone willing to share his life, and not be a secret about his family.

It was strange and such a mind game: Ralph must have been feeling some type of way since I hadn't been calling him nor asking to see him. I still cared for him and no matter how nice it was to have met Isaiah, I realized I was still in a relationship with Ralph. This one particular night he called me. Of course, I rode out West to go see him. It's something about when we saw one another—it's like a magnet or electricity that goes through my body. Ralph had a way of touching me that I've never experienced in my life. And when we made love, it was passionate. Real. The way he held me, kissed me… my body just released explosions too indescribable to explain. The sex wasn't for minutes. No, we had sex for hours and hours. We never tired and he always stayed erect—how was that possible, I don't know. We could be finished, and in the next minute, he'd touch my back with a full erection. Our sex drive was truly unbelievable.

Is this why I stayed with him? Is this why we both stayed with one another? I didn't believe this was LOVE. Did we believe having sex made us stay with each other? Or did the sex just draw us closer? I'm here with Ralph, but my mind was with Isaiah.

Sure enough, my phone began ringing and I couldn't even answer. It was Isaiah calling me. We would have talked by now. Isaiah knew all about Ralph though I hadn't spent much time with Ralph. Lately, I was always hanging out with Isaiah and Samantha. Not sure why, but Samantha had no clue that me and Isaiah were talking over the phone or hanging out late at night in front of his house sitting in the car talking all night.

Fast forwarding with me and Isaiah. Our relationship was getting real now. I'm with two men I haven't slept with Isaiah just yet (remember: when you know, you know). But I was definitely enjoying our time hanging out and talking. It was a Friday night, and I was home alone. Per our usual routine, I gave Isaiah a call. He told me he would be hanging out on the block—whatever that meant. He invited me to come through if I wasn't too busy to sit with him while he played cards at a friend's house. Isaiah was great in playing cards. He always would win. I told him I would let him know though deep down; I knew I was on my way to the block. I went to the corner liquor store to grab me a bottle of wine. Yep, I was back to socially drinking—nothing hard though. I went back to the house, thinking to myself *Nope, you're not going to meet this man. You're in a relationship. You're going to take a hot bath, make you some popcorn, call your Ralph and see what time he will be getting off work, and maybe he can come over afterwards.* This was the plan. I picked up the phone and called Ralph multiply times. Of course, no answer. I figured he was working late and that he'd call me. It was now after 11 p.m. and Ralph still hadn't called. Time to swerve; I decided to call Isaiah back. I had finished my whole bottle of wine, plus ate the popcorn and was feeling myself. Isaiah gave me the address and I got dressed and met him over there. They weren't doing anything but drinking, playing cards, and talking trash. Isaiah offered me a glass of his drink—something strong like tequila. I politely declined. The other guys in the house were talking about going to this hole in the wall lounge located down the street. Isaiah told them we'd go for a little while.

Everyone headed out to the lounge. Isaiah knew everybody in there. I couldn't remember the time we left, but we stayed until they closed. I was a little more than tipsy at this point, and I asked Isaiah if he needed a ride home. He said, "I don't think you'll be able to drive me. I don't know how I'm getting home since my friends are leaving with females and I can't call Samantha since she's out with a dude."

Slightly slurring, I smiled at him and said, "Come stay in my guest bedroom." My daughter wasn't home with her twins for the entire weekend, so her room was available. Isaiah ended up driving to my apartment, which wasn't far in Englewood. He even helped me up the stairs. I shouldn't have ever drunk a whole bottle of wine, plus drink tequila that he was drinking. I showed him where the guest bedroom was. Being such a gentleman, he helped me undress, and then he laid down in the guest room. That wasn't good enough for me. And I knew what I wanted. Instead of staying in my room, I went into the guest room and got into bed with him. Everything went down from there. Was he resisting me? At some point, I believe he told me no one time. I asked him a few more times. He finally gave in to me. I got what I wanted. Was it right? No, but when you know what you want, you go after it.

The next day came, and I apologized for my behavior. Why did I do it? I guess to get back at Ralph for not being there. Weeks began to pass by without me even noticing Ralph hadn't called. I believe he knew something was going on, but just couldn't put his finger on it. Instead of waiting on his phone calls, I was enjoying hanging out and spending time with my friends. We even started having hang-out nights at my house, and bowling nights with friends and family. Things between me and Isaiah began to get serious. He broke down to tell me about this case that he was coming up against and that he would probably be going away. I couldn't believe what I was hearing: the man that I've grown to care for will now soon be going away to prison. NO GOD. Not this man. If I were ever having a bad day, he would wash my hair, massage my feet, cook dinner, run my bath water, watch my daycare while I ran errands...he was my constant in my life. WHY GOD?

Isaiah explained to me what happened and how he got caught up, and if he went to prison, how long he would serve. At this point in Isaiah's life, I felt like I couldn't leave his side. Every time he went to court, I made it my business to be right by his side, never leaving him, even at every hearing. Each time he needed to see his lawyer; I was there for him. I didn't care about anyone else not being there for him. I knew that I was going to be there for him.

One night, Isaiah's older sister was having an event at her house and he wanted me to come. I couldn't believe this: I had been with Ralph how long now— five or six years? I repeatedly complained to him how I wanted to meet his family, and he never brought me around them.

Then this man came along, and I got to meet his family after four months of hanging out. I had met his sisters; and he'd even shared stories about his children, his mother, and his entire family. His actions showed me a lot. And my dumb-ass kept getting sucked into Ralph's sex trap. What the hell was wrong with me holding on to Ralph?

I felt so much love at Isaiah's older sister's birthday party. Everyone was so friendly. I had a ball laughing all night, playing cards and drinking wine while Isaiah maintained his drink of tequila. I met his older sister and baby sister too. I'd learned so much about his family, and how they loved to have fun and said whatever was on their minds. Ralph had never given me this type of love by sharing his family.

After the party, we headed back to my house and stayed up all night talking. It wasn't about the sex with Isaiah. It was more than that. He made me feel special around him and he cared about my well-being. Although he felt this way about me, this happiness between us wasn't going to stay. He would end up changing later.

Taco night was a Saturday night and Isaiah had

his girls this particular weekend. All our friends were coming over to play cards, listen to music, and the kids would play games as well.

Samantha came over but was acting strange, but as the night continued, her attitude changed. No one knew me and Isaiah were messing around, except for my best friend of course. Isaiah played cards and trash talked like he always did. We hung out late into the night. Everyone that knew me, knew I got sleepy around 9 p.m., but I'd hang as long as I could. Just like a big kid I got sleepy. The next thing I knew, it was 3 a.m. Five in the morning, Samantha decided to head home, and she was willing to take Isaiah and the kids home. I told her it was no need and that I'd take them home. The kids were in the guestroom sleep, which meant Isaiah would have to sleep in the room with me. I mentioned this to him and told him "I'm still in a relationship."

"You're not in a relationship with Ralph. He ain't been coming around. He doesn't even know anything you're doing. He barely calls you. How can you say you're in a relationship with him?" I didn't care what Isaiah was saying. I held firm to the fact that I was still holding on to Ralph. I didn't even understand why. Was it the sex? We barely saw each other. Maybe I held onto Ralph because I knew Isaiah would be going to prison. And I didn't know how long he'd be gone. Truth be told: maybe I was afraid to be alone.

On our bowling night that we set up with our family and friends to hang out, we had planned on telling Samantha that we were officially together. I don't know why we didn't tell her from the beginning. Bowling night was a hit. Everyone's laughing and drinking. Before we could tell Samantha about our relationship, someone else spoke up! They just busted out like "Why you and Kesha keeping secrets? Hey Samantha, did you know Isaiah and Kesha were tighter?" I didn't know what to expect when she heard it blasted out from someone else and not us.

Slightly shocked Samantha smiled. "Together? No they aren't." We busted out laughing and told her we'd been together for at least three months now out of seven months. She couldn't believe how she didn't see the signs. Samantha was cool with everything and every day after that day, we three were back laughing and hanging out together all night long.

The more time we spent together, the more our families were introduced to our relationship. One night after we were coming back from Samantha's house, I had to stop by my mother's house before dropping Isaiah off. I asked him if he didn't mind us stopping by my mother's and since I had met everyone in his family, it was time he met my mother. The moment my mom saw him, she said exactly what my best friend said. "This young man truly likes you and cares for you." Their conversation wasn't long. My said it was the way he watched me and the concern in his eyes when he was around me that stood out to her where she knew he cared for me.

"I could feel the compassion from him," my mother said. She had never said anything like this about anyone that I've ever been with. I knew exactly what she was talking about. I knew this man cared for me. But how is it that someone can care for you this way and then turn around years later and hurt you? Down the road, Isaiah plotted to hurt me because of my love for Ralph. I just didn't know it was going to happen.

Can you love two people? Yes, you can. It's so possible and I was in that place that I had LOVE for Isaiah, for his well-being. And on the other hand, I'd always been in LOVE with Ralph. I wasn't sure how I got caught in this triangle.

The next time I spoke to Ralph, he sounded so sincere about his love for me. He wanted things to work out between us, and he promised he would spend more time with me. We had been down this road before. I wanted to be on the road to him introducing me to his girls and family. I was already at this place with Isaiah. Whenever I hung out at family functions, Isaiah's family knew who I was and treated me like family. Isaiah had so much charisma and personality. My family enjoyed him being at our family functions. We always had fun hanging out with the kids, going out on dates, playing cards, and sharing in so much laughter. Isaiah's court dates went from monthly appearances to weekly court appearances. I was so worried about Isaiah. I was not going to leave his side. I wanted to be as strong as I could in this situation. The lawyer he had sucked.

Isaiah became highly stressed out, drinking every day, and hanging out until late every night. He tried to spend more time with his children and explain to them what he knew was about to happen. He didn't know the outcome, but I believed in my heart of hearts, he knew he'd have to serve time. On the way to the final court day, we drove silent in the car. As we walked into the courtroom, we held hands. The lawyer awaited us outside the courtroom. I could see Isaiah's face trying to hide that he was not ready. His mother, her boyfriend, and one of his best friends was present to support him. We entered the courtroom. They called his name and my stomach dropped. I was trying to hold back tears because I knew this day was coming. The judge reviewed his case and announced the sentence. My ears felt clogged up. I couldn't believe Isaiah was found guilty.

Swiftly, the officers clinked handcuffs on him. All I could think was *Nooo*. He was trying to tell us something as he was getting escorted away, but I couldn't read his lips. This was horrible. I'd never experienced this before. I've always visited dudes in jail, but to actually be by someone's side in the courtroom was a new experience. The lawyer gathered us back into the hallway and explained things to us.

I was angry and didn't want to speak with the lawyer because I felt he didn't do his best. As I left the courtroom headed towards my car, I couldn't think. I couldn't breathe. I sat in my car and I just cried uncontrollably. My heart fell to the floor. My friend——he's gone for who knows how long. I didn't know when I'd hear from him or see him. this couldn't be happening to me.

Days turned into weeks and nobody had heard from Isaiah. I had been keeping in contact with his mother, best friend, daughter, and Samantha. All I could do to keep busy was focus on my daycare business and look for a house. I had been temporarily staying with my mother since my building in Englewood was no longer safe. I would check the website every day and made sure I was available if he happened to call. I also collected money from friends to put on his books. I was excited to learn from his mother that he was in the county jail for a few months until they transferred him. A relief came over me once she told me about Isaiah. I was there the first day he was able to have a visitor. I couldn't wait to lay my eyes on him.

The day of our visit, I waited for hours to get a 20-minute visit. Walking in a room with thick glass, waiting for him to come out of a room. We smiled and our eyes were focused on one another. We talked and laughed. I was so concerned about him, but he told me he was doing well and he gave me instructions to handle some things he needed done. I also told him how much money was collected. He couldn't wait until he left and to get his time over with. He'd use the time to do a lot of thinking.

As I awaited to hear from Isaiah, I finally found a house. All of a sudden, after months had gone by—Ralph came back around. He called me every day. Something was different now. Talking to Ralph was a waste of my time. We had nothing to talk about. Or was I comparing him to Isaiah?

Isaiah and I wrote every day. I looked forward to

reading his letters and we were now telling one another that we loved each other. The further he was away from me, the more I missed him. I took pictures of the house and mailed them to him. I explained to him what day I would be driving to see him, and that six hours away was not going to stop me from driving to see him, even if I had to drive by myself. On this trip, me and his older daughter would come to see him. The drive would give us time to get to know one another.

The day arrived for us to visit him. We headed out early around 3 a.m. in the morning. We would be able to sit for three hours or maybe longer and talk, eat some snacks, and catch up. Then he could see his daughter and spend time with her, which was great. When we saw him, all I could think and say out loud was "Wow, you're so small." He smiled and hugged us both. We sat down, talked, laughed, and ate lots of snacks. I couldn't believe that I was looking at him. The time didn't go by fast; it was just right. Before we left, he said, "I will be seeing you soon. Be sure to write." He smiled and hugged me tight, rubbing my back. After that visit, I made every effort to see him once every month by myself. We would have a great time talking. I remember him telling me that he would be home soon. Three years was becoming too long. I told him that I couldn't wait any longer. I don't know why I was being wrong and selfish. No man wanted to hear that kind of talk knowing that he's locked up. Especially from the woman that's supposed to be by his side. The woman couldn't give up.

When the day arrived where I received a telephone call stating Isaiah was home, I thought he was playing. But when I found out Samantha was picking him up from Union Station, I knew it was real. Isaiah didn't call me and that hurt. But why should he? In his last months of prison, I told him that I wanted out. I wouldn't want to be bothered with myself either. When I received his call telling me to come and pick him up from his mother's house, my heart just smiled with gladness. Isaiah wanted to see me, and I was happy because it showed that he still cared for me. Or did it? When we saw each other, we both smiled and hugged one another. I took him to my house and gave him a tour and he was so happy for me. We talked, laughed, watched movies and spent the whole night together.

Fast forward two years later. I don't know how I kept being with someone who was always emotionally abusing me, tearing me down with words, and belittling me. "You're just a blonde with a small brain." Isaiah had completely changed prior to being locked up. He constantly brought up Ralph's name in arguments. I never denied Ralph, and he always knew of him and my love for Ralph. But I hadn't even been with Ralph. How could someone that said they cared about me keep saying such horrible things to me?

I would overlook the words not realizing that he was tearing me up emotionally. Isaiah changed and I didn't know why he kept bringing up Ralph's name. Why was he so intimidated by another man? I did not know. He constantly claimed Ralph had my heart. I thought Isaiah's root frustrations came from the fact he didn't have a job, or maybe it was something else going on. In due time, things would be revealed.

During this hard time for Isaiah, Samantha and I would help. Isaiah would hustle, but it was never enough. He was getting frustrated by his finances. Unfortunately, no matter how much Samantha and I helped, Isaiah became more verbally abusive. I started overlooking him belittling me saying that I was "Kesha, who has half of a brain to think for herself." Or he'd say, "Oh Kesha, you're just a blonde." I would laugh it off, and then it would come to the point where I would start believing him. I started saying these same things about myself to people, apologizing for mistakes, and then I would say, "I'm just a blonde." Isaiah was hurting. He would always accuse me of seeing Ralph. I ignored him, and assumed he was misunderstood and hurting. But what was really going on was that he was hurting me verbally and I just dealt with it. The abuse was worse when he drank.

He would bring up the fact we weren't being sexually active, and that I was going out West to spend time with Ralph. Or that I was talking to him over the phone. I would bring the drinking to Isaiah's attention, and he would claim he didn't drink every night, which was a lie. He was in denial. I guess he was trying to convince me or himself. I began second-guessing myself. How could I be so stupid?

This man had so many insecurities, damaging whatever was left of our relationship. We were growing apart. No more late-night talks, movie nights, spending time with Isaiah's friends. No more of his loving family. All of that was fading away.

Never ignore the signs. When someone says something, they mean exactly what they are saying. Isaiah would always say, "Everybody uses somebody."

Memorial Day weekend. The time had come for the truth to be revealed. I was out with Isaiah's sister and I had noticed that he and I hadn't talked to each other all day. Hmm, this was strange. We decided to take a ride. This was the first holiday we were not together. That was a sign. Around 1 a.m., we rode past their mom's house just to see what was going on—well looka here, looka here. Guess who was standing outside talking to a young lady? You guessed right—Isaiah. As we pulled up, he came to the car, asked us what was up. He claimed he was outside talking with a friend that he hadn't seen in a minute. I could tell that this girl—more like a "child" since she was the same age as my daughter—wasn't just a friend. Her disposition told me something else. His sister wasn't paying attention to the signs, but I was. "How long you plan on being out here with your friend?"

"Not long."

"I'll be back to get you. I'm about to drop your sister off."

Quickly, Isaiah says, "Oh no, Kesha go home. I'll catch up with you tomorrow."

"Uh-huh, yea ok," I say. I dropped his sister off without saying anything. I went back to his mother's house and he's still standing outside with this girl. I didn't want to give them much space in my book. I parked, got out of the car, and asked what was going on. The girl told me not to direct my attention to her. She was totally correct. I asked Isaiah what was going on as he began to walk away. He's trying to tell me not to make noise since it's early in the morning and his mom is asleep. Freaking bum. I'm getting pissed off because the girl told him to let me know what was going on. She knew my name, the vehicle I drove, everything about me. She then told me that he didn't want me.

Confused, I'm looking dazed. Isaiah kept telling me to leave. I left to pick up his sister. We came back. His sister couldn't believe that her brother-best friend kept this from her. Isaiah's sister kept asking, "Who is this girl?" The girl said that they had been tight for three months. I finally left.

I was shocked and hurting at the same time. I couldn't even explain why I was so hurt or even shocked. Later, Isaiah and I decided to meet and talk about why he was messing with this young girl. He confessed that he did all of this because he wanted to hurt me for the years I was with Ralph and was not loving him. This was his way of getting back at me.

Wow. It was amazing to see how he could plot, plan and be so evil. He used me for years. All because he had insecurities about another man who had no clue of who you were. I felt it was more to this story. He called me a liar. "What did I lie about? I never denied or lied about anything." It's always two sides to a story.

He wasn't happy with me and he wanted to leave but didn't know how to. So being with a younger girl that didn't have anything but babies, made him feel superior. He felt like he was winning. I tried for a few months until August to make things work. But Isaiah felt like if I had him and Ralph, why couldn't he have me "to use" and the young girl sexually? I couldn't put myself through that type of companionship. He was at a place in his life where he needed someone to use and I was in a place in my life that I needed companionship.

I wouldn't say it didn't hurt losing him. What hurt the most was the wasted years. And it hurt that someone belittled my character because of their own insecurities.

As months passed on, I found out so much about Isaiah from my family, friends, and his family. Things were beginning to add up about certain situations. It was so hurting that this man tried to tear down my character. I couldn't believe that people I loved allowed him to do this to me; they all said they didn't want to say anything because they knew I cared for him. Isaiah was turning friends against me with his lies—because of what he was doing with his new girl in order to keep me away from certain people. He couldn't stand me.

His day would come—Karma was real.

CHAPTER SEVEN: Finding my Self Love

I remember sitting in my living room with the rain hitting my windowpane. I had many sleepless nights, constantly crying. I would wake up at 2 a.m. in the morning and sleep would not come to me. One morning, I decided to just get dressed in all black. I grabbed my house keys, and decided to walk from 103rd to 111th. As I arrived at Isaiah's house, I was watching him with his new girl sleeping in a tent in the backyard of his mother's house. Instantly, thoughts rushed through my head to just grab a bat and smash in both of their brains.

But no, God kept me from going to jail or just blacking out. I heard his voice clearly: KESHA. I kept thinking *Nobody would ever know it was me*. I kept telling myself that I had too much to lose.

If I hurt them, who would care for my daughter and grandkids? I wanted him to pay for all of the men who hurt me, tried to destroy me. I wanted him to pay for all the men who abused me physically, mentally, verbally and emotionally.

That night, I just walked away. I would do this every night for a month until I couldn't do anything else. I felt as if prayer wasn't helping, neither was writing in my journal. I needed help— counseling.

It seemed as if the men I had been with all had similar characteristics. I used my alone time to process what I needed to do. I needed time for myself to rethink, rebuild, work on my self-esteem, focus on myself and my business.

I can say that it was very difficult. There were many painful nights, crying and not understanding. I can truly admit that I had many nights plotting to destroy someone just because they not only destroyed me mentally but played on my kindness.

ACKNOWLEDGEMENTS

I want to thank God for giving me the opportunity to share the life behind my journey. With his love, joy, forgiveness and peace guiding me through. I truly want to thank my backbone and role model: my mother; my daughter Angelica who inspires me with her strength; my siblings whom I truly love; Auntie Barbara for encouraging me; Henry, my Godfather for his true love; my Miracle Twins who inspire me to keep living; and to my family &, friends: I thank you all for your love, prayers, and support.

~Fretful, my Angel I miss you and love you.

(He was the definition of a real man)

www.ingramcontent.com/pod-product-compliance
Lightning Source LLC
Chambersburg PA
CBHW072357030726
47505CB00014B/1877